Thornton J. Hains

Richard Judkins' Wooing

A tale of Virginia in the revolution

Thornton J. Hains

Richard Judkins' Wooing
A tale of Virginia in the revolution

ISBN/EAN: 9783337027445

Printed in Europe, USA, Canada, Australia, Japan

Cover: Foto ©Andreas Hilbeck / pixelio.de

More available books at **www.hansebooks.com**

RICHARD JUDKINS' WOOING

A TALE OF

VIRGINIA IN THE REVOLUTION

BY

T. JENKINS HAINS

(AUTHOR OF "CAPTAIN GORE," ETC.)

F. TENNYSON NEELY
NEW YORK AND LONDON
1898

Richard Judkins' Wooing

CHAPTER I

I was sitting in an arm chair with my feet upon the hand rail of the verandah —very much at my ease — when Major Bullbeggor rode around the bend of the turnpike and came into view.

I watched him lazily and noted the action of his mare's hind feet as she threw little jets of dust off to either side. The jets mingled together and formed a yellow cloud in the rear, through which could be seen the grinning teeth of Snake in the Grass,

the Major's nigger, who always acted as hi
body-servant. Snake was mounted ungracc
fully upon an old spavined clay bank, anc
he came loping along some three or fou:
fathoms behind his master.

The sky was cloudless and the warm sun
shine appeared to annoy the Major.

I was so comfortable, sitting there witl
the buzzards soaring in silent circles over
head and listening to the small birds sing
ing in the shrubbery on the lawn, that :
had just made up my mind to hail th(
horseman and ask him to accept the hospi
talities of Judkins' Hall—and all who hav(
been anywhere in the state know the repu
tation of my house — when the single
footing mare turned sharply from the mai

road and came loping up the carriage drive toward me.

I might as well tell you now, that the Judkinses were never of a nervous or excitable temperament. Even the first Richard Judkins, Earl of Belldon, and viscount Ansley, was noted for his cool and calculating disposition. But if you think I am overstepping the bounds of courtesy by dwelling too much upon the characteristics of my family, I will say that I only do so for fear someone may hear this who is a stranger in the colonies, and who might, therefore, get a wrong impression of the manners bred in and taught to a Virginia gentleman.

As I said before, I am not nervous ; so I

sat calmly watching the Major and his servant until they halted within ten feet of the soles of my shoes.

"Good morning, Major!" I cried, "How are you to-day? Jump down and come in!" And with that I took down my feet and rose to greet him.

The Major's face seldom relaxed its grave expression, although he had a sympathetic eye, but this day he looked more stern and military than ever. His dress added to this effect, for he now appeared for the first time in the uniform of Woodford's irregulars, with a long, straight sword dangling from his broad belt.

He stroked his pointed, tuft-like beard which hung from the end of his chin, and

wirled his long, grey moustaches, while his
eyes looked from one object to another as
f searching for something. Then he saluted,
saying, "Is there a Prince George county
nigger about here, Mr. Judkins?"

Snake in the Grass bent forward in his
saddle, and I noticed a thin, rod-like contrivance rise from the back of his coat collar
and lift off his hat, replacing it again the
instant he sat up straight.

"Yes, sir, there is. Here, Sam!" I cried,
and my boy stepped out from behind a
corner of the house and stood attention.

"If there is," continued the Major, "he
can hold my horse a few moments while
Snake, there, takes up my left stirrup a

saddles are built, and I'm certain this one will be the death of me yet. It has already given me trouble in my left knee joint."

I gave a look at Sam who sprang to the Major's bridle—and I might say here, that for an all-around good nigger, my boy Sam was hard to beat. He stood six feet one inch on a pair of ham like feet and weighed two hundred weight. He was a black, big-limbed, bullet-headed, broad-faced, hog-nosed nigger of the pure Guinea breed, and he came from the best stock in Prince George's—but that goes without saying, for the Major would rather have seen his favor-ite mare struck with a whip than in care of any other but a Prince George nigger.

"Well, sir, how do you feel, and what is

the news to-day?" I asked, as I stepped down from the verandah and shook his hand when he had dismounted.

It was always the custom to ask Major Bullbeggor how he felt, for although he was only fifty, or but little over twice my age, he always appeared to be suffering very much.

"I feel a little better than I did last week," he answered, "but I have some pains shooting all through me, sir. Yes, sir, a pain, now and then, a shooting all through me. I've been taking Miranda Jones' spring medicine, but it don't seem to do me much good. I'm quite certain there's a settling in my joints, coupled with a numbing of the nerves and twitching of the scalp. Dr. Mc-

Guire bled me twice last week and drenched me three times—but no matter, a soldier has no time to devote to talking about his physical sufferings, even if they are unwarranted News I have, unless you have seen Roger Booker to speak to while he was riding an express to the assembly at Richmond."

"No!" I answered, "I've not seen Booker since last May, when he went with you to help organize some of the colonial companies. But what has happened? No more of that rioting and massacre like the affair of Concord and Lexington, I hope?"

The Major walked slowly up the steps and seated himself comfortably in the arm-chair I had just occupied, and then waited patiently until I drew up a chair and was seated. I saw he had some important news, but, of course, was not discourteous in my haste to find it out. The Major had served through the entire French war with Colonel George Washington, and was a man of the most pronounced military method in all things. It would have been showing a gross disregard for his training had I even suggested that he should hurry and tell me what was uppermost in his mind, before he had thought carefully upon the proper manner and time for doing so. For himself, he was most punctilious, at all times, in his manner and address to gentlemen of his own rank and station. He was sometimes truculent of speech, but he even went so far into the matter of politeness and good breeding that when his trusty body servant, Snake in the Grass—he always had a humorous way of naming his people—forgot to bow properly and remove his hat on one or two occasions, he had the rod-like contrivance rigged upon the slave's back which lifted and replaced his hat as I have described. The idea that Snake was a lazy, shiftless nigger, never entered the Major's head. Snake may have been a good servant, but for my part, I've always stuck to the old method of training one's people and have seen more than one Prince George county nigger all the better for a little dressing with a small hickory switch; especially when extenuating his circumstances.

My cousin, Will Byrd, who was a few

years my senior, came out of the house on hearing us talking, and, after greeting the Major, had a small table brought within easy reach. Upon this was placed a bottle of brandy, some sugar, ice and sprigs of young mint.

The Major sat there silently stroking his beard while Will mixed the beverage, nor did he even offer my cousin a suggestion, knowing well the mixture that had been famous in Judkins' Hall ever since the days my grandfather and Lord George Fairfax honored its roof.

But because we held our English ancestry dear, and observed their customs, don't think that we were rank tories.

Will and I had both been friends of Lord

Dunmore, before he started his aggressive policy, but since then we had had little to do with him. We also held aloof from the too radical followers of Mr. Patrick Henry. That is, from all except Major Bullbeggor. The Major had been my father's friend, and since his death had always been a welcome visitor at the Hall, even though he had helped to raise a company sent to Boston, and had joined Colonel Woodford's militia.

Berkley Harrison and Captain Barron were in the breakfast room talking to my mother and sister. They had just finished lunch. Harrison was an outspoken tory who lived upon the adjoining plantation, and who, though only thirty years of age, was one of the richest planters on the James river. My mother had a high regard for his many accomplishments, for he had lived much in England, and had the bearing of a man who had seen something of the life at His Majesty's court.

Therefore Will and I were anxious to hear what important news the Major had to tell before anyone else joined us, for we were afraid lest his radical views should reach the ears of Mr. Harrison.

When the Major put down his glass he looked at us, and it was strange to note the effects of the liquor in the old soldier's face. Every line, from the heavy creases about his square jaw to the fan-like wrinkles that stretched away from the corners of his eyes, seemed to stand out more clearly. His eyes brightened and he spoke with great feeling —

"Gage's men stormed the hill defenses at Boston last week, and carried them by assault," he said.

"The devil," said Will.

"And then what happened?" I asked, jumping from my chair.

"What could happen with a lot of yokels against regular troops, hey? What could happen? But," he added, and his eyes fairly flashed, "our boys made a fine stand, sir. Yes, sir, stood there on Bunker Hill 'till the last dram of powder was burned, and the scoundrels were running in and jabbing them with the bayonet. Yes, sir, by Gad, sir, they have the making of the finest men in them that ever stood up to be killed."

"I wish I had been there," said Will.

"Wish thunder!" roared Bullbeggor, half rising from his chair. "What's the use of wishing! Why don't you do something besides lying around here and wishing. Holy thunder! If I was your age I would have been there in the thick of it with our company of Prince George boys. Wish to thunder!" And the old soldier reached for the bottle.

"That is as may be," remarked Will, quietly, referring to the Major's imaginary military movements.

"Wish smoke and blazes!" growled the old fighter, putting down his empty glass.

"If it was'nt for this settling in the bones
and numbing of the joints, and having pains
shooting all through me, to say nothing of
a vertigris in the head when I stoop over,
I'd have gone up there with the boys. As
it is, I'll do what I can against that rascal
Dunmore,— and stay here with Woodford
toe do it."

"But give us the details of the Boston
fight," I urged.

"That's all I know," he answered. "I
met Booker riding an express to Richmond,
and he told me just what I've told you. I
think you and Will here would be welcome
at Woodford's—if you don't want to go so
far from home — and he will give you
enough fighting before the year is out. But

isn't that Berk Harrison's voice I hear? He's hand and glove with Phripps and Dunmore, and, perhaps, he would not care to hear my sentiments on the affairs of the day."

"Old Captain Barron is in there with him," said Will, motioning with his hand toward the room. "It's nearly two, so they ought to be through breakfast and be out in a few minutes."

"There isn't a better soldier than old Barron alive, although he places too much value in the small sword and pistol—two worthless weapons for real fighting—Ah !"

At this instance the figure of Berk Harrison appeared, issuing from the window of the breakfast room, which being cut level with the floor within enabled anyone to walk out on the verandah. He was closely followed by Captain Barron and my sister, Mary. Harrison was dressed with his usual care, wearing a buff waistcoat and snowy ruffles. Although he had slept in the Hall over night, he had not appeared in the breakfast room until after I had finished my midday meal. He wore his hair carefully queued, and his lean, smooth face, with its arched eyebrows, aquiline nose, and thin, straight lips, bespoke the cynical man of the world — and also of fierce passion.

There was a hard glint in his eyes the instant they were directed toward the Major, but the glance softened a little when he noticed me.

"Good morning, Major Bullbeggor," he said, advancing toward the old soldier, who rose to greet him. "How are you, sir, this morning?"

"Pretty well, thank you, sir; yes, sir, pretty well, considering a little settling of the bones I probably got by riding too long yesterday—Ah! Good morning, Miss Judkins." And then he shook hands with my sister and Barron. The Captain and he had served together and were old friends.

"Always well and hearty, Barron, eh?" he cried.

"You see, Miss Judkins, the difference time makes with men. Here's Barron sitting around all the time with the ladies as young as he was twenty years ago, and just look at me—a perfect wreck, yes, Miss, a perfect wreck. I shouldn't wonder if he began to think of getting married next—if he only had a pension, eh."

"My face ought to be worth a thousand a year to any woman," laughed Barron, drawing up a chair, while Mary stepped down from the verandah to pet the Major's mare and have a word with his strangely attired nigger, Snake in the Grass.

"Your face, indeed, ought to be worth that, Barry," continued the Major, smiling at him thoughtfully, "but it is a question that might admit of some diversity of opinion among women, in comparing it to the relative value of affections."

"It is strange that women should put

such a value on such things as affections,"
said Harrison, smiling at me, "but self
esteem is to be commended in the sex."

Barron laughed heartily, as he always did
when jokes were made at his expense. He
always laughed at, and took a light view of,
everything, and it was this that made him
so popular with the young people, for he
was, physically, the ugliest man on the
river. He refused to wear any hair except
his own, which consisted of two little red
tufts just over his ears. These latter stuck
out from the sides of his head like a pair of
fans. His face was full, bronzed and rugged featured, and absolutely hairless, and
his mouth curled up at the corners in a per-
petual smile. His great, red nose was

almost purple, and its color, he claimed, had cost him much time and money to develop. He was short and stout, but always wore the baggiest of brown homespun breeches.

"Women are not the only persons who like comfort," said he, and the Major, very thoughtfully, passed him the bottle.

"No, no," he cried, motioning away the liquor, "I never drink at this time of day, and very little now at all. Only a bracer or two when I rise, then another before eating, along with two or three in the late afternoon—and a couple before dinner—and—well, I'll take just one, if you insist."

"Its easy to see that Barron's heart lies in his stomach," said the Major. "There's an old woman's saying that 'to win a man's esteem, you must feed the brute.'"

"And, likewise, to win a woman's, 'dress the animal,'" laughed Barron.

"But what was the news, Major, from Boston? I thought I overheard you say something about a fight," asked Harrison.

"He did," said Will. "Gage's men carried Bunker Hill by assault, last week. But he says the Virginia boys fought well and gave the reddies all they wanted."

"They did that, and Woodford's men will give Dunmore about the same, if he doesn't bear a hand and leave," interrupted the Major sententiously.

"You don't say!" laughed Barron, raising his glass. "Well, here's to the army of Virginia, and may it reap much benefit from the Major and his combination of Christian men."

"And have reason to give thanks that they'll be in no worse condition than that which they find themselves," muttered Harrison, putting down his untouched glass. "They'll be damned lucky if they're not."

"Oh, well, it is hardly necessary to be profane about it," said the Major, quietly.

Barron smacked his huge lips and smiled blandly, then murmured softly—

"And when they pawned and damned their souls
They were but prisoners on paroles."

"An apt quotation," snapped Harrison ill-humoredly.

"You don't look as if you were much given to poetry, especially Butler's."

"An angel is sometimes disguised as a devil," laughed Barron.

"But never as a soldier," said Harrison, dryly.

"Nor as a fop," growled Bullbeggor, "which the same might be said of some people who dress to appear like gentlemen, but about whom there might be some diversity of opinion among men." And he looked straight before him.

"Your wit is coarse, and if you mean that for me, I'll say you are damned insolent," said Harrison with some energy.

"Oh, hold on!" said Will.

"The Major did not mean that for you," I said quietly, advancing toward Harrison, who stood leaning against a pillar of the verandah. "He never makes rude remarks to anyone," I continued, trying to pacify his rising anger, "and he simply meant the *vice versa* of Barron's jest."

"I don't overstep the rules of politeness very often," said the Major, slowly, "but I don't believe in fitting all cases to a set of rules. It is better sometimes to make a rule to fit a case, such as this, for instance. If Mr. Harrison thinks I made the remark for the purpose of comparing him to an angel, he is most unaccountably satisfied with his personal appearance and certainly flatters himself, but if so, he is welcome, and be damned to him. I'll give him whatever redress he wishes at any time. Only I'd rather take it out of his friend, Dunmore, if —"

"Hold on, Major! You forget yourself," cried Will, placing a hand on his shoulder.

"I'll see that you make good your words to-morrow morning, old as you are," said Harrison, now white to the lips with passion. And he walked away and down the steps, meeting my sister Mary, who had just heard the raised voices and had turned to see what had happened.

"Why do you waste time talking to those old men," I heard her say as they walked together down the path which led to the grove of live oaks that separated the estates. But he appeared not to answer, so I knew there was trouble ahead.

"Harrison has horrible taste to get angry at such an old fellow as you," laughed Barron. "Also a pretty clever opinion of his presence."

"I am old, Barry, sure enough, but I can't abide a man who lives in a country as a gentleman and then fights against it. I've got these pains shooting all through me and considerable twitching of the skull, but I'll meet him, sir; yes, sir, I'll meet him to-morrow morning if I'm alive. I offer you my humblest apology, Mr. Judkins, for being party to a scene on your verandah, but you heard what he said in regard to soldiers, sir; yes sir, you heard what he said." And the Major reached for the bottle, while I entered the house to leave again by a side door and follow Harrison to do what I could to pacify him.

Will Byrd was living with us, so I felt sure he would keep Barron and the Major in good humor until I came back.

Mary met me on the pathway leading to Harrison's. She had just left him and was much upset at his temper.

"I don't see why you have these old duffers come up here and make trouble," she said. "Captain Barron is bad enough by himself, but when that horrid old Major Bullbeggor and he get together, they just sit around to drink and make trouble. It's only an hour's ride to his place and I don't see why Sam can't help Snake take him home."

"My dear sister," I said, "you know the traditions of Judkins' Hall. The Major shall, therefore, always be a welcome visitor. He is a good soldier, and the time will come—if it is not here already—when Virginia will need just such men. We cannot put up with Dunmore's violence any longer, and if Berk Harrison can't understand this, the sooner we see less of him, the better it will be for us all."

"Good soldier! Huh!" she cried, with a pretty toss of her head. "If Virginia depends on such men for soldiers, my lord Dunmore will soon settle the disturbance. Good soldier, indeed! Why it was only last week he and Captain Barron were sitting up drinking and telling their abominable adventures, and they were anything but a soldier-like kind. Poor Mrs. Bullbeggor overheard them and has threatened to get a divorce. Snake said she had hysterics, and kept screaming that her husband was fit for

nothing but paying bills. Good soldier, indeed!" And Mary went into the house
with an air of indignation that would have
done credit to a queen—or a Judkins.

I went over to Harrison's, but on the way
I couldn't help wondering if this power to
pay bills, which Mary held in such high dis-
dain in the Major, was not just a little at-
tractive in young Harrison. Women have
strange methods of reasoning out the proper
way to look at things.

Harrison declined to see me, at first, but
after I had sat out two cigars on his verandah, he appeared.

He refused to listen to any peaceful over-
tures that I advanced, and I wasted all the
afternoon and evening trying to settle mat-

ters without a meeting. His friend Phripps
dined with him and afterwards left with a
formal challenge to the Major, requesting a
meeting at sunrise the next morning. I left
Harrison at about nine in the evening, after
an uncomfortable meal, with the feeling
that trouble was in store for the Major.

On reaching the Hall, I found dinner over
and the Major and Barron in bed. The
Major had requested Barron to act for him
and had accepted the challenge. They had
settled upon a spot down on the river shore,
and all who know the James will remember
how flat and smooth the shore is at this
bend.

The fact that there was to be a meeting
had been kept secret from my mother and

sister, for even Mary did not think the last words she had overheard meant anything dangerous, but, in spite of this, it was easy to see that the house servants suspected something was wrong.

My mother gave me a lecture about the advisibility of taking her advice, and also how to treat the Major. She really liked the old soldier, in spite of his eccentricities, but wished, also, to avoid offending Harrison I forget now just what the advice was, but, as a matter of course, had I taken it, all must have ended well, for time and again afterwards have I heard her affirm this—so also has she in regard to other matters.

I walked out on the cool lawn under the bright stars, and then around the house, hoping to find Will who had stepped over to the stables. I met him as he was coming back and together we walked around behind the slave quarters, discussing the affair of the Major's and also the gloomy outlook of war in the colonies. The news of Bunker Hill had affected both of us greatly. As we passed an angle of the house we heard voices.

"Is yo' sho' nuff a Prince Gawge nigger?" said one.

"Dat I is, honey, sho'; an' I's de nigger uf er Prince Gawge man," answered the other.

"Kin he stan' agin Marse Berk?"

"Doan make no moan, honey, dere'll be bluddy murder an' suddin demise in der mawnin'."

CHAPTER II

Just before daybreak I was suddenly aroused by the violent movements of the Major, who occupied a room next to mine.

The bell-cord was pulled viciously for some moments, and this was followed by hoarse exclamations.

Finally someone answered the bell and knocked at the Major's door.

A. deep grunt followed and the door was partly opened.

" Are yo' a Prince George nigger?" asked the Major, sleepily.

"No sir !"

"Then git out and send me one right away."

The door closed, a short period of silence followed, which was suddenly broken by more violent pulls at the bell cord. Then I thought I recognized Sam's footsteps sounding softly along the hall, and the door opened again.

"Are yo' a Prince George nigger?" grunted the Major.

"I is sir, " came Sam's answer.

"Then for the Lord's sake take a look around and tell me where I am at."

"You'se right heah, Major. Right heah, sah. "

"I thought so," said the Major with a satisfied sigh, and as the door closed again a long drawn snore told plainly that he had relapsed into peaceful sleep.

I was too much aroused, by this time, to sleep any more, so I lay awake thinking of the possible dangerous outcome of the meeting that would soon take place.

Soon I heard footsteps again approaching along the corridor, and I was then aware that Barron and Will Byrd were approaching the Major's room. It was barely daylight, but I jumped up and dressed and made my way into the room to join them.

The Major was still undressed. He sat on the edge of the bed and appeared so nervous that he could hardly put on his clothes.

This amused Barron very much.

"Its' no use, Barry! you know the old saying about the dogs' hair being good for his bite," said the Major, throwing down his clothes. "Gimme some of the hair, and I'll see if this twitching of the bones and numbing of the nerves don't hold off a bit. Lord! I didn't drink anything last night to amount to anything. I was just a little tired out riding over from Pendletons."

Barron poured out a good, stiff drink of brandy, and the Major gulped it down without winking.

Then a most remarkable change came over the old fighter's grizzled features. He jumped up, and in less time than it takes to tell of it, he had his clothes on, and was just buckling on his sword belt, when Barron stopped him.

"Now, Bull, whoever heard of fighting a duel in such a rig," he cried. "Take it off, man. Byrd has the tooth-picks for this work," and he pointed to a couple of rapiers, wrapped carefully in cloth, that Will carried under his arm.

The Major looked from one to the other of us.

"Fight a duel!" he cried in astonishment. "Who in the name of six sons of Hayman is going to fight a duel?" and he forthwith strapped on his sword-belt.

Barron burst into a fit of laughter. "Never mind, come along with us. But where on earth, Bull, did you think we were bound for at this hour in the morning?"

"Think!" roared Bullbeggor, " I know I'm going to ride to Williamsburg and re-

port to Colonel Woodford. Think thunder."

Will looked a little disgusted, but said
nothing, and I led the way softly down the
corridor and out the back way without
awakening my mother or sister.

The Major looked about him with blink-
ing, sheeny eyes for his mare. Not seeing
her, he started for the stables, calling out
lustily for Snake in the Grass.

Barron seized him by the arm and stopped
him. "Bull," he cried laughing, "youv'e
made an appointment to meet Harrison,
and he is waiting to get a clip from you
down on the shore. Don't make any more
racket, but come along before you wake up
the household."

I must say, I was somewhat disgusted with the Major's behavior, so I spoke out, telling him he would have to meet his man.

"Meet him!" he bawled, turning on me fiercely. "Of course I'll meet him." Then he turned toward the stable. "Snake!" he cried, as his nigger appeared, "Get the mare ready, for I'll be through in a few minutes. Lead the way, Mr. Judkins. Meet the devil!"

I then led the way down to the river bank, just as the rising sun tipped the tree tops with golden light.

The shore in the bend was very flat and sandy, being overhung partly with great, sweeping willows. As we neared the spot fixed upon we were aware of the presence

of Harrison and Phripps.   They were standing under a large tree and appeared to be
much absorbed in conversation.

As we approached them they turned about,
and Phripps advanced, holding a pair of
small swords in one hand and a case containing pistols in the other.

Will and the Major stood aside and
Phripps, Barron and myself proceeded to
arrange the details of the meeting.

It was decided to fight the affair with
swords, until one or the other of the com-
batants was completely disabled, and I must
say that Phripps was fair enough in the
matter.   He measured the weapons and
gave Barron the choice, after which he took
the one left and started toward Harrison,

who had strolled down on the river shore
to where the sand was hard and firm.

I might say here, that I was not at all
unfriendly toward Harrison, and that I only
took part in the affair after I had done
everything in my power to settle matters
peaceably. It required nice discernment, in
those days, for a man to make up his mind
whether he was a tory or not, and it was
more because I sympathized with the
Major's political ideas, than anything else,
that I took any part in the matter at all.
As it was, I acted as I had acted several
times before in such cases ; that is, as referee
or judge, while Barron and Phripps were
seconds to their respective men. Will
Byrd simply acted as a spectator. It was

a perfect spot for a meeting. The tall
sweeping willows for a background on the
low bluff-like bank, and the water spark-
ling in the sunshine beyond the shadow.
The sand of the shore was firm and flat, and
there was plenty of room, as it was now
nearly low water. I marked a spot and
gave the signal for the men to take their
places.

I introduced the Major to Phripps and
bade Barron hand him his weapon quickly
to avoid unnecessary delay, for I knew his
habits of inquiry.

"Mr. Phripps, your mother was a Robinson, I believe, if I remember correctly,"
said he, as Barron passed him the hilt and
cast off his sword belt.

"I never met her as a girl," snapped Phripps, impatiently.

"The more honor to her," replied the Major, quietly, as he flashed out his heavy broadsword. "No fear," he continued, as Phripps reached hastily for the pistol case, "I'll attend to you some other time. I have to do with Dunmore's heel dog first."

I took up a pistol and cocked back the flint. "You know the penalty, Major. Take your place and weapon," I said.

He looked steadily at me for a moment, his eyes gleaming with a strange light. Then he answered :

"This is a weapon I've used for some years past, Mr. Judkins, and it is the only one I will use in this quarrel. If no one cares to meet me my mare is waiting to carry me to more important matters. Take the devil!" he growled deeper, "I'll take the stiffening out of somebody."

"Don't disturb him on my account," spoke Harrison. "Let him use his weapon and talk less. I make no objection to it at all. I am ready." And he took his position.

I looked at Phripps, but he nodded approval; so I gave the word to begin. I heard Barron laugh out some remark at the Major's expense, as the men stood on guard for an instant. Then the fight began.

As I said before, I had already seen some sword play and indifferent marksmanship on that beach, but this affair was most uncommon.

The men were at it fiercely as the weapons fell across. Harrison, with gleaming eyes and a sneer of contempt on his lips, thrust and lunged past the broad blade of the Major's with cat like quickness. But to no purpose. The Major, holding his heavy broadsword as lightly as a rapier before him, with its scabbard held high in his left hand behind his back to keep it from his knees, turned each attack by a slight, strong turn of the wrist. His face was grave and calm, but as I watched him, the gradual tightening of the muscles in his lean, bronzed jaws showed that either the strain was beginning to tell on his wind, or else his temper was rising rapidly. However, he refrained from attempting the stroke I knew must soon be made, unless Harrison jabbed him.

The morning was warm and soon the perspiration was pouring down the faces of the men. Harrison eased up a moment to note his effect on the Major, and seeing that he was keeping him in hand, pressed forward again with vigor.

Backward went the Major, giving ground slowly in a circle, while that look of surprise I have seen on more than one man's face, when suddenly confronted by grave danger, spread slowly over his streaming features.

Harrison was getting white and waxy about the lips, and his breath came in loud rasping gasps, but his eye was like the glint of steel as he pressed fiercely on.

I have never seen a better swordsman. His wrist began to tire, but he instantly passed his hilt to his left hand and then came on harder than ever.

I looked at Barron and saw the smile go from his face as the Major circled backward past him. The old soldier's left hand was holding his scabbard lower and lower, until finally he dropped it entirely. Then Harrison saw his time had come for the finish.

Quick as thought he passed his hilt to his right hand again, for the final thrust through the Major's wavering guard.

Then happened the most uncommon thing about the whole affair. It was done so quickly my eyes could hardly follow it, although I was standing but a few paces away and looking directly at the men.

As Harrison passed his hilt to his right hand, the Major's weapon fell to the right of him with his foot still advanced, and as Harrison lunged strongly, the Major's broadsword rose and fell with a wicked "swish."

Harrison's sword passed neatly through the Major's shoulder and protruded fully a foot behind him, while the old soldier's weapon struck Harrison fairly on the head and stretched him limp on the sand. The heavy blade had struck close to the hilt, as he had lunged forward, otherwise it must have bitten in as deep as the eyes. As it was the blow was bad enough, and we rushed in to see what could be done for him. It was several minutes, however, before he opened his eyes and showed any signs of life.

While we worked to stanch Harrison's wound and revive him, the Major walked off a short distance and sat himself on the edge of the low, bluff-like bank beneath a willow. He then carefully stripped off his new uniform before Barron or Byrd thought of leaving Harrison to come to his assistance, tied up the rapier thrust, and prepared to move along in the direction of the Hall with his sword belt slung carelessly over his arm.

When Harrison's wandering gaze met him his strength came back suddenly, and it was all Barron and I could do to hold him in check. He insisted that he should continue the engagement and Byrd's outspoken objections only inflamed him the more.

The Major suddenly glanced back and saw what had happened, so he halted while Phripps ran toward him.

"The affair is not quite over, if you please, sir," said Phripps as he approached.

"Isn't, eh!" grunted Bullbeggor, drawing his sword and throwing the scabbard aside. "Then if you can prove that your gentility consists in something more than a love for horses and dogs—and women, you can get your hand to some weapon." And with that he came quickly forward.

"After Mr. Harrison has finished with you, we can go further into the matter with some advantage," said the second, motioning with his hand towards his principal.

But Harrison's strength was unequal to

the occasion. He no sooner stood alone than he wavered, staggered, and then pitched forward on his face in a dead faint. Phripps quickly ran to him and raised his head while I poured some brandy between his lips.

The Major stood silent and motionless before the group, his sword point resting upon the toe of his boot and his hands crossed over the hilt. A strangely grave and thoughtful expression shone on his rugged face, now perfectly calm from the heat and excitement of the fray; and as I watched him he appeared to me a poor duellist, and a man to whom self was not the all important realization in life.

I went toward him and held out my hand. He took it in an absent minded way and

turned at the sound of approaching footsteps behind him. I looked over his shoulder just as Snake broke through the fringe
of willows, leading the Major's mare by the
bridle.

"I suppose he isn't hurt badly, Mr. Judkins," said Bullbeggor, looking at his limp
adversary. "But even if he is, I don't believe I can do much for him. I thank you,
sir, for your hospitality and fairness. I
must go along now, for I'm due at Williamsburg before night."

"You certainly will come back to the Hall
and let us fix you up a little, Major. You
certainly must feel a little shaken from that
puncture. It may be more dangerous than
you believe," I said.

"Not at all, sir. Not at all. I have had
Dr. McGuire bleed me twice as much in the
last month. I do feel a slight twitching of
the bones and a sort of dead feeling in the
nerves, but besides a few pains shooting in
and out, I'm all right. Then there is Pendleton's tavern at the cross-roads a mile beyond the bend, and you remember the old
rake keeps good bottled stuff. No fear, I'll
be all right. But I will take a small drink
with you, Barron and Byrd, just to show
there's no hard feeling."

Harrison had begun to show signs of re-
turning consciousness, so Barron and Will
left his side and came forward a pace or
two. The flask was passed around and then,
in spite of Barron's protests to the contrary,

the Major insisted on carrying out his plans as he had already intended. He buckled on his sword belt and mounted his powerful mare, while Snake plunged into the bushes and reappeared a moment later mounted and ready to follow his master. His black face was showing in marked contrast to the white gleam of his huge mouthful of teeth, and it was evident that he had viewed the fight from some unseen point on the river shore and was well pleased with the result.

We raised Harrison and carried him in the direction of the Hall. In a few minutes he revived and looked about him for the Major. Not seeing him, he insisted on walking the remaining distance to the house on foot and we finally allowed him to attempt it.

Just as we crossed the road, opposite the driveway, I saw Snake in the distance turn sharply in his saddle as we came into view. Then, through the dust cloud that almost instantly swallowed him up, I noticed his head bend outwards and his white cap rise and fall in an ungraceful bow.

CHAPTER III

The second day after this meeting we were at breakfast, sitting somewhat stiffly at the table, when my boy Sam, whom Mary had just sent over to Harrison's to find out how he did, brought a note in answer, saying that he had almost entirely recovered and hoped to have the pleasure of meeting her that morning. Barron and Will were still staying at the Hall and we had all been somewhat reserved in manner in spite of the old Captain's jests. Although there had been no serious outcome to the affair, a meeting of that kind, no matter how common the occurrence, always makes women a little distant and cold in manner to the parties concerned. This is possibly because a woman is somewhat more civilized than man, and anything that savors of brutality or fierceness, always is more revolting to her than to the less artificial being.

I have said the occurrence of such affairs was common enough in the old days, before the practice of putting grooves in pistols and making them as accurate as rifles to a steady hand, became general. After that men became more careful about abusing the code and getting into scrapes, for the pistol has always been recognized as a weapon for gentlemen in Virginia. But I must confess, however, that meetings have always been numerous enough, and for the most trivial causes, on the soil of the grand old commonwealth.

After Mary had read the note from Harrison she became much more civil to Barron, and even my mother's stern dignity thawed a little under the prospect of a renewal of social intercourse with the master of the Harrison plantation.

Mary was only nineteen, and although southern girls are women of that age, she possessed a great deal of that childlike simplicity, which is, or is not, so acceptable to the majority of men. For my part, however, I have always been ungallant enough to believe that a woman affects much.

Will had been devotion itself for two years past at Judkins' Hall, for he lived only a few miles away near his family's old country seat at Westover, and consequently found it quite easy to see the inmates of the Hall several times a week even when living at home. He was my favorite cousin, and it was almost painful to see his spirits as much affected by my sisters' as a barometer is by the weather.

"Why don't you say something," she said to him, after reading the note and watching the quiet, grave look on his face.

"What shall I say?" he answered, smiling with her, "I'm here to talk to you." And in truth he did appear to be always around for that purpose, but never able to raise his voice to the occasion.

"I don't know whether you are or not. I've been reading about a man who carried on an affair simply by whistling. But even that would hardly apply to you after taking part in that duel. You certainly would hardly care even to whistle to me, or you would not have gone with them. Perhaps you are here to eat and fight."

"You invited me to breakfast."

"Yes, but that does not presuppose you are too hungry to speak. Perhaps you think I asked you here to see you fight, and then satisfy your hunger. You don't know why I asked you here. If you are here to talk to me, do say something. Why did I ask you here to breakfast?"

"Words are sometimes used to convey ideas," I suggested, trying to help Will along, for I well knew how little women care for a man who can't say something light and foolish at the right time.

"Or to conceal them," said Barron, breaking in with his old saw.

"But where the ideas are vague and not quite well defined, what then?" asked Mary, with a knowing look at her mother.

"Then I don't see how they can be of any value, whatever, and I don't see how I'll ever find out the true reason for my being here, though I'd much like to know,' said Will.

"Quite right, Will." said my mother smiling, "I don't care for vague ideas either —or to hear a man and woman in worthless gibble-gabble, gibble-gabble. If there is a dearth of ideas, one reason is as good as another."

"I admire silence, also," laughed Barron,

"for there is an old saying in regard to its value. But at the same time, give me plenty of plans, schemes and feasibilities."

"I like the latter well enough myself," said Will, so dolefully that we all were forced to smile, and my charming sister laughed outright, saying—

" Certainly Captain Barrow's conversation is not lacking of ideas, but then he is a blunt man, and plain, so it is hardly to be expected that he should conceal such scintillating wit"—

" Blunt man,—and soldier, if you please," interrupted Barron, with intense gravity, seeing his chance to heal the rupture between himself and Mary.

"I may add, 'and soldier,' when I see

some evidence to justify it," retorted my sister with a little energy. But Barron only laughed and we finally adjourned to the verandah in a more civil mood than when we sat down to breakfast.

The air is delightful on the river at this time of year of which I speak, and, as you probably well know, has a soothing effect on the nerves, for it is not at all cool, nor is it hot enough to excite the circulation.

We sat there in the delicious, fragrant breeze for some minutes before we were aware of the approach of Berkley Harrison, Phripps and Miss Rose Carter, a cousin of Harrison's.

Miss Carter had come over with her maid to nurse her cousin the moment she had heard that he was hurt, and as Harrison lived alone, except when some one like Phripps was with him, a woman would have been a good person to have had at hand, had he been injured badly, or had my mother and sister not spent most of their time attending to his wants.

I suppose I might as well say, before going further, that although I am only a poor Virginia gentleman who has nothing but his—well, estate and inheritance—I had some hope of raising myself to a position from which I might allow my gentler passions to have some sway.

You will understand what I mean when I tell you that for beauty of face and figure, coupled with a grace beyond description,

Miss Carter was—well, I will not tire you with details that are so well known. And then, again, a woman's beauty depends entirely upon her attractiveness to a man, and some men will see beauty in one way and some in another; never all alike. Why, I have seen the niggers in the slave quarters let Harrison's house servant, Angeline,—a yellow girl of remarkable beauty,—pass by unnoticed and then, ten minutes later, be peeping and spying at the blackest moke wench that ever left the Guinea coast.

Harrison's greeting, this morning, was a trifle cool to Barron and myself, and his appearance was not improved by the sinister look of his shining black eyes. These were somewhat sunken in his pale cheeks and had dark crescents beneath them. His head was bandaged, but a skull cap covered all signs of his wound. To Will Byrd and my sister he was most gracious, and he even bent his wounded head to kiss the tips of my mother's thin fingers.

"You see," he said, after Miss Carter and Phripps had made their greeting, "I took the opportunity to come over to tell you that Lord Dunmore has sent word that he fears great trouble in the tide-water districts, and that all the gentlemen of the province were making ready to embark on his vessels and leave with their families until the insurrection is more in hand."

"And when will that be?" asked my mother in some alarm,

"Oh, only a few weeks, at the most," said Phripps, breaking into the conversation.

"Yes, about that time," continued Harrison, "but you know how fanatical such men as Bullet and Bullbeggor are. It's really absurd how much influence that beggar, Patrick Henry, has over such ignorant men. The man has about as much logic in his discourse as a nigger has in his, but he sways his followers any way he wishes, and is gaining recruits every day. I suppose you know how illiterate the fellow is ? "

"And how rough and ill-bred, "said Miss Carter.

"An ill-favored rogue and no mistake," said Phripps.

" Odious men — vulgar ruffians, all of

them," said Miss Carter and Mary together.

"So you say!" murmured Barron, pleasantly.

"And their followers are a pack of unhung thieves," added Harrison fiercely. "No house is safe while they roam the outlying counties"——

"Mercy!" quietly interrupted my mother, who felt very kindly toward the revolutionists, "One would actually suppose, Mr. Harrison, that you were quite unfriendly with the whole party."

And when she finished speaking I could see Harrison's eyes fairly blaze with anger. He was very quiet, however, for some moments, and then adding that it would be well to be packed and ready to embark with

Lord Dunmore when he arrived, he turned to my sister and talked of other matters.

Barron waxed flippant and jolly while talking to Phripps, so when everybody was in good humor I took the opportunity to ask Miss Carter to help me hunt thistles — for my mother.

We walked some distance through the fields, and found few thistles, but among other matters discussed were certain characteristics of Mr. Berkley Harrison.

"The most accomplished and perfect gentleman in the province," said Rose.

"But, my dear Rose, he is so uncommon vain"—

"By which, I suppose, you mean simply that he has a decent opinion of himself, owing to his birth and position," she interrupted. "A man who hasn't a proper opinion of himself, seldom has one of any of his friends or acquaintances."

"Quite true," I answered, "but "—

"Do you really object to him so much?" she broke in. And as she smiled and blushed slightly I followed the direction of her look and saw Mary and Harrison standing together at the corner of the box-hedge of the driveway.

"You could hardly expect a gentleman of cousin Berk's antecedents to agree with the absurd ideas of government you pretend to," she continued.

"The matter is possibly open to discussion," I answered a little stiffly.

"Oh, no offence, my dear Dick. You know the laws of human nature as well as I do. Those who are governed and have little are always antagonistic to those who govern and have much, no matter how perfect that government is."

"Yes, I know," I answered, "there is no such thing as justice in this world. Even the Bible, most holy of records, disclaims it, saying, that those who have little shall have that little taken from them and given to those who have much. At least that is what I make of it, but even if there should be a small minority to govern and grind a large majority, the majority should have its representatives to see that no unjust "—

"Nonsense!" she interrupted, "Those

who represented it would soon acquire the same habits and tendency as the minority, without even the leavening of high birth and education the minority already have. There are some people born with high ideas who are intended by Providence to govern always. They are superior in feeling—but hush! What is cousin Berk doing?"

We were now close to where Harrison and Mary were standing, and I noticed that he peered cautiously over the hedge at some object that lay on the other side in the sunshine. We turned the angle of the drive way and as we did so I saw my boy, Sam, lying at full length upon the grass, looking quietly up into Harrison's face with an expression of curious interest showing upon his black features.

"Are you busy, Sam?" asked Harrison softly, not noticing my approach.

"Yessah," replied Sam without moving.

"Eh! What?" and I saw him grasp his cane firmly in his hand behind his back,

"Yessah," continued Sam, "I'se been lying here fo' quite a spell, sah, listenin' to my heart beatin'."

"So, so," said Harrison quietly, measuring his distance. Then he flashed out—"You infernal, impudent nigger!" And he smote Sam a crack over the head that brought him to his feet with a wicked look in his eyes.

"Superior feeling!" I muttered angrily, and I saw Miss Carter blush. Then stepping further out into view I caught Sam's eye in time to avert further trouble, for he had never been handled before by anyone—except, perhaps, myself.

"Go to the quarters, Sam," I cried, and as I did so I saw Harrison start at the sound of my voice and notice me.

I would have given something to have seen what Sam intended to do after that look,—for he was a big, black, powerful, hog-nosed nigger, capable of some little mischief—but the ladies being present, such intentions were, of course, impossible. Sam obeyed me instantly and went quickly toward the stables with his broad shoulders well squared and his head up, and Harrison continued on his way with my charming sister upon his arm.

"I suppose," I said, looking askance at Miss Carter, "this is the superior feeling of the governing class which we have just witnessed?"

"What would that black boy have done?" she said, in alarm. "I saw the look in his eyes that certainly meant more than disobedience."

"Oh, Sam is a true and trained Christian," I answered, somewhat nettled at the scene. "I taught him the doctrine of forbearance myself and I have seen him practice it to some advantage."

"And what was that?" asked Rose, sweetly, looking up at me with her lovely violet eyes that still showed traces of her alarm.

"Well, the last overseer I had was a man of superior feeling who belonged to the governing class—and he started to govern accordingly. He smote Sam savagely upon the side of his bullet head, one day, and knocked him down. Sam jumped up and rose to his full height, offering the other side of his head without so much as a word. The fellow, John Smith, struck him again, like a fool, and stretched Sam senseless for half an hour."

"And then ?"

"Oh, then Sam came to, and as soon as he could stand, he drew his corn knife and it was all we could do to keep him from killing that overseer. As it was, he got so badly cut that he would never come back again to the Hall."

I saw Miss Carter pale slightly.

"Are many of your people so brutal and blood-thirsty ?" she asked.

"Sam is neither one nor the other, but as good a boy as ever followed a gentleman"—

"For revenge, do you mean ? If that is so, I think the sooner I tell Berk—Mr. Harrison, the better."

"Oh, Lord, no," I cried, "I mean as a servant. Even Major Bullbeggor allows him the privilege of serving him, and you know how particular he is. But why so anxious about Berk Harrison's welfare ?"

"I am his cousin," answered Miss Carter, stiffly.

The tone of her voice was enough. But Heavens ! A man must take his strokes, mental or physical, without too much wincing. As for me, I like the man who can meet them with a smile on his lips and talk in a steady, natural voice while his heart stops beating and the iron grip of sorrow holds his throat like a vice. The tone of Rose Carter's voice, that day, told me something in regard to cousinly feeling. But no matter. Our greatest sorrows are not nearly so heavy some years afterwards and—

As I said, I felt a sensation, similar I now believe, to that which a few others have felt before. But a man in love is never a philosopher—and he is generally hasty and selfish.

"I congratulate you, my dear Rose, on

your relationship," I said coldly, and the blood rushed through her face and left it whiter than before.

"Do you know, my dear Dick, you sometimes bore me most stupidly?" she answered. And this commonplace incident ended.

Commonplace it was indeed, but what it meant to certain affairs which happened afterward, you may judge, if you care to listen. It is the little commonplace affairs that influence the lives of most people, as anyone may remember who cares to look at the past.

CHAPTER IV

Dunmore failed to appear the next day, and Harrison came over to the Hall and had the pleasure of the company of both Mary and his cousin to beguile him.

Will and I, accompained by Barron, whom we persuaded to join us as a sort of spirit raiser, took our fowling pieces, a pair of good dogs and Sam, and sought distraction in the covers below the bend. It is astonishing how sympathetic young men of good antecedents will become under certain circumstances. I always liked my cousin Will, and it seemed to me now that my sister was cruel, and he a much abused friend, since Miss Carter and I had had a sort of understanding between us. But no matter, Will and I had always been drawn together, and our silent companionship was very soothing and restful in spite of Barron's incessant story telling and irrational humor.

The old soldier had followed around all day without so much as firing his piece, which he insisted on having Sam carry with the flints at full cock—much to my boy's disgust. I had always taught Sam to be careful with weapons, but Barron insisted on readiness above all things, and would not allow the flints down. We had bagged several brace of fine birds while he was engaged in other matters, and after seeing that Will and I were having all the sport he wished to have his weapon ready but still refused to carry it. Twice there had been premature explosions, the last of which tore off the rim of the old soldier's hat, but, after each discharge, he made Sam reload and proceeded on his way, tranquilly spinning story after story in high good humor, and avoiding anything that might ruffle the feelings of young men in—well, say in an uneasy, or perhaps diseased state of mind.

We tramped along all day, and late in the afternoon we were to the eastward of the bend and making our way slowly through the heavy timber towards the river in the lower reach. Will was slightly in advance of the rest of us, and as he broke through the thick fringe of cover near the river bank, he gave a sudden cry of astonishment and stopped. Sam promptly caught the lock of Barron's gun in some undergrowth and instantly exploded it, much to our annoyance, as it peppered my favorite setter severely and sent him howling down the river shore with a dozen or more small shot sunk deep in his hide.

In a moment we cleared the pines, and the first thing that met our gaze was the *Fowey*, frigate, close to the beach and standing up the river with all her working canvas set and her guns run out ready for action. Behind her came several smaller craft, apparently crowded with men and guns. One glance at the ship told plainly who she was, and upon her high poop strode a man fore and aft whom we had no difficulty in recognizing as Lord Dunmore, His Majesty's Governor of Virginia.

We were less than half a mile distant, but the shadow of the pines made it much more difficult for those on board to see us, half concealed as we were in the long grass and low bushes, than for us to see them. The poor dog, however, howled dismally, and the report of the gun was evidently mistaken for the discharge of a hostile rifle, for in a moment a great cloud of white smoke burst from the frigate's broadside, and the same instant the air seemed alive with grape-shot, while the jarring report of a

twenty pounder echoed along the shore
The balls tore with a loud, ripping, rush
through the pine tops and crashed through
the undergrowth. One of them striking
the butt of Will's gun smashed it to bits and
knocked him endways into the woods.

To say we were a little surprised at this
reception would hardly describe our feelings. I made a spring for cover and hugged
a large tree trunk as though a storm were
breaking over me, and as I did so I heard
Sam give a yell and disappear as if the
earth had swallowed him up.

It was over in less time than it takes to
tell of it, and I stepped out to see Barron
laughing heartily as he dragged Will to his
feet.

"They do make a most valuable noise," he laughed, "but there's little harm in them. The devil! You were lucky in not getting that into you—mere chance though." And he picked up Will's shattered gun.

"If that's the reception Dunmore is going to give us, I think we might as well keep on to Williamsburg and join Mr. Henry's men," said Will, looking somewhat disturbed in mind. "I never had a high opinion of his lordship's manners, but this is going it a little too far. I wish I had my rifle, I would see if he would do a little jumping at the crack of it. Here, Sam! Give me the Captain's gun and I will load with ball and have a try at him."

"Is it over, Marse Dick?" asked Sam's

voice coolly from somewhere in the thick bushes.

"Come out, you black rascal!" "cried Barron, and presently Sam emerged from cover rapidly reloading Barron's weapon, at the same time keeping an eye on the vessels as if expecting an attack.

"Don't do anything foolish, Will," I said, as I saw his temper rising, "It is a serious matter to fire on His Majesty's Govenor. Besides, here comes a boat from the first schooner to inquire into our affairs."

While I spoke, the vessel close in the frigate's wake luffed sharply, and as her headway slackened, a gig full of soldiers, pulled by four stout niggers, shot away from her side and came rapidly towards us.

Then the vessel tacked ship and stood slowly in after the boat, her head sheets slacked off to stop her headway and the black muzzle of a long twelve pounder sticking half a fathom clear of her forecastle rail.

We stood in a group on the sand and awaited developments, supposing, of course, that as soon as we were recognized the vessel would proceed on her course in the wake of the frigate.

Dunmore we all knew quite well, for he had been several times to the Hall and had often visited Will Byrd's cousin at the magnificent estate at Westover.

As the boat load of soldiers neared the shore the schooner luffed again within easy hailing distance, and a man standing by the forecastle gun hailed us.

"Throw down your arms, you dogs, or I'll blow you off the ground!" he roared.

"The devil!" exclaimed Barron, "I wonder if he means that for us? But our dogs are not armed."

"Bang!" went the long twelve pounder in a cloud of smoke, without another moment's warning, and a shot whistled over the small boat and struck the beach a few feet in front and to the right of us. A storm of sand and gravel drove into our midst, staggering and blinding me so that I fell against Will, who in turn fell to the ground, swearing furiously.

A small particle had struck him with great violence in the eye, and in his fury at this brutal onslaught he sprang to his feet, grabbed my gun from my hands, before I had recovered sufficiently to stop him, and fired a load of small shot slap into the boat full of men just as its keel touched the sand. A perfect roar of curses followed, as the soldiers received the scattering charge. Then Barron seized Will, and just as several men leaped ashore with their guns raised to shoot, all three of us were struggling on the ground. Sam, left alone to face the loaded muskets, dropped Barron's gun and instantly disappeared with a couple of musket balls snipping through the brushwood after him. The next instant we were surrounded by men and dragged to our feet, while a short, but big-limbed Irish sergeant stood near and gave orders to his crew not to bayonet us.

"Who are you, and where's the rest of you?" snapped a grizzled, lean-faced officer, running up with his sword drawn and looking full at Barron.

"I am Jameson Barron, Esq., sir," said the Captain, smiling pleasantly, "and as for the rest of me, I believe it is in Richmond. Dr. McGuire cut it off the day after Braddock was killed and put it into a small flask of alcohol." And he held up his left hand from which the last finger was missing.

"None of your jokes, sir," snapped the officer. "Where's the rest of your party?"

Barron looked about him.

"Sam!" he called loudly. "Sam!"

"I guess he's taken the track," he continued, quietly, "but must still be within a mile of us. However, before we go too deeply into the case, sir, you will oblige us greatly by stating your authority for firing upon gentlemen who are in no way hostile to His Majesty."

"Yes," I said, "I am Richard Judkins, o Judkins' Hall, sir, and am well known to Lord Dunmore. By what right do you fire upon us while we are simply out shooting for sport." Here I looked around for our bag and ammunition flasks to prove the statement, if necessary; but Sam, who had been carrying almost everything, had run into the bushes before dropping his burdens, and they were out of sight.

The ammunition left us was not of a character to corroborate my statement to any degree of exactness. It consisted now of several musket balls that Will had put in his pocket for use in case we had met larger game.

"Sport, eh !" snarled the officer, rubbing his shoulder where a shot had penetrated the skin. "You'll see sport enough before we get through with you. You may start on them, sergeant."

He turned away abruptly on saying this, and, with half a dozen men deployed as skirmishers, proceeded to examine the edges of the forest for traces of a hidden foe.

"So 'tis sport ye're afther, hey ?" said the sergeant. "Give yourself no oneasiness, ye'll see it fast enough. Rooney, me sowl, lay yer hand tinderly on yer trigger, while I investigate the handsome old un, an' if he so much as winks his ears, blow his tripes out, d'ye see?"

Barron made no further comment, except to inquire of private Rooney what particular part of his anatomy held the "tripes" alluded to by the sergeant.

"Hold yer tongue, ye handsome old man,' said that officer. "My sowl, but ye have a dacent figure av a soldier, despite the years av yer cocoanut. Fancy him, boys, squinting wan av thim oies av his at a leddy," and he ended with a hoarse chuckle, while he carefully went through Barron's pockets.

We were each examined in turn, but nothing of a hostile nature was discovered,

except Will's half dozen bullets.   These,
with our tobacco and snuff boxes, were carefully tied up in a handkerchief and carried
by the sergeant to the boat.   Our guns were
also appropriated.

The officer in charge returned presently
from his search along the shore, and having
found nothing in the shape of a foe, he ordered all hands into the boat.

I protested with some energy against this
high handed proceeding, but was instantly
seized by several soldiers while another
stuck his bayonet point half an inch into
my back.   Will was treated in the same
manner, and Barron, knowing resistance to
be useless, set us the example by walking
quickly to the boat and climbing aboard.

In a few minutes we were on our way to the schooner.

As we drew near, I noticed the vessel's peculiar rig. She appeared light in the water, with long overhang fore and aft, and her masts raked backwards to the last degree. Her spars were long and tapering, and new, while her bulwarks appeared to have been built up to the height of a frigate's, showing that she was evidently some fast vessel altered and fitted up for the work Dunmore had planned on the river. Four ports cut in her broadsides held the black muzzles of her battery of light twelves, while on the forecastle was the pivot gun of heavier metal, which had been discharged at us a few minutes before. Men swarmed

on her main deck and about her battery,
while small knots stood with the sheets in
hand ready for further orders.

The man who had hailed us from the forecastle, and had fired without further warning, now stood at the starboard gangway,
where a hanging companionway trailed in
the water. He wore a shabby uniform,
such as I had seen some of Dunmore's officers wear when doing their so-called patrol
duty on the river. He was short and stout,
with a red face, his shifty, fishy eyes looking like two little gray dots on either side of
a nose that much resembled a boil.

As we drew alongside he bawled out
orders, the men hauled flat the head sheets,
and instantly the schooner began to forge

ahead. Some one threw a line and a man in the boat caught it, making her fast at the companionway, up which the officer in charge of us scrambled to the main deck. We were quickly sent aboard, followed by the boat's crew, and were lined up in the gangway between a file of soldiers, while the small boat was dropped astern to tow in the vessel's wake.

CHAPTER V

We were slightly bewildered at the rapidity and novelty of the events which were happening, and for some moments I stood and gazed at the hurrying men, who appeared to obey a man with a shrill whistle whose notes rose and fell with long undulations. No misunderstanding seemed possible, for each note appeared to mean an order, which sounded high above the rattle of the vessel's gear. I was something of a yachtsman, and took great interest until aware of the presence of the stout man with the red nose. He was in command of the schooner, and he now stood before us, gaz-

(103)

ing at us as if we were wild animals of an unknown kind. Two or three younger men in the group that gathered about us appeared to be officers, but I had never met any of them before, so they joined their captain in his curious gaze. Finally the Captain spoke.

"Mr. Rose," he said, in a thick, raucous voice, "are these the men who fired on us?"

"Yes, sir," replied our thin faced captor, holding the handkerchief containing our valuables in one hand, while he saluted with the other.

"Then what d'ye mean by bringing them aboard this vessel, sir?" he roared. "Haven't I told you, sir, to shoot every rebel caught with arms on him? Hey! Answer me that, sir! Answer, or I'll break you sir!"

"They claim to be gentlemen, Captain Cahill," said our captor, meekly.

"Blast you! Do you mean to disobey me, sir? Answer my question, sir, or by breechins and blackskin I'll break you sir!" roared the captain.

"Yes, sir; yes, sir, you did," answered the lieutenant, quickly. "You gave me orders to shoot every rebel caught in arms, who refused to surrender. But these men claim to be gentlemen and not rebels. This one," and he pointed to me, "claims to be a friend of Lord Dunmore's."

"Claims!" roared the Captain, getting almost purple in the face, and it really

appeared as if he were going off in a fit.
"Claims !" And then he simply drew in
breath for a moment to gather power to
express himself. Here was an opportunity,
I thought, so I broke in—

"Yes, sir," I said, "I am well know to
Lord Dunmore, and also to nearly every
gentleman on the river. I am Richard
Judkins, of Judkins' Hall, and I"—

"Shut up !" he roared. "Don't you
speak to me sir. If you do I'll cut you
down where you stand." And he drew his
sword. "You may be Richard Perkins,
of Perkins' Hell, or any other hell, but if
Lord Dunmore knows you he knows an
unhung scoundrel. Don't glare at me, sir ;
don't glare at me that way, or I'll cut you

down where you stand," and he advanced a step towards me.

"I am a Virginia gentleman, sir, and I demand to be treated as such," I said.

"You are a liar and a villian," he roared, "and I will treat you as such," and with that he made a pass at my head that would certainly have finished me, had I not jumped suddenly backwards into the arms of a soldier behind me. At the same instant Will Byrd sprang forward to ward off the blow.

He caught the skipper's sword arm with his right hand and instantly dealt him a powerful blow just under the ear with his left. It sent the man to the deck as limp as a rag, with his sword clattering after him. The next instant Will was seized and thrown down and a line quickly passed around him, lashing his arms to his sides. Then Barron and I were served likewise.

The Captain lay on the deck as if dead, so in a few moments he was picked up and carried below to be nursed back to consciousness. In the mean time the schooner had been standing up the river under all sail, with the breeze abeam, and was rapidly nearing the frigate that was sailing under easy canvas to allow her to catch up and report the news of the affair on the shore.

"Carry the prisoners below in the forehold," ordered Mr. Rose, who was now in command, and we were quickly carried down through the forehatch into a dark, ill-smelling hole filled with bunks and all sorts of ship junk, and there we were left with a couple of men to guard us.

I stretched myself comfortably on a coil of rope and awaited developments, thinking, of course, that the instant Dunmore heard our names we would be released.

"It's no use, we are in for it," said Barron, smiling, "I only hope we will catch up with the frigate before Captain Cahill recovers from that tap. Very neatly done, Will, most remarkable—if it had been a trifle further forward though it would have made a pretty mess of things — Hello! What's that?"

We were on the weather side of the

schooner, and she was heeling over and going through the water at a great rate. The rush of the waves was quite loud and continuous against the vessel's side, but above the noise I could hear a hail from somewhere in the distance to windward. Then came an answer from the schooner's deck—

"Three men!" bawled Mr. Rose from somewhere above us. Then came another hail.

"Don't know," bawled the Lieutenant in reply. "One named Perkins, of Perkins' hole."

Then came another pause followed by another hail.

"Two young—one old, with a face like

the breech of a brass carronnade—all alive and well—no one hurt."

A pause.

"Didn't suppose you knew them"—

Another pause.

"Will not hurt them, sir"—

Then came a pause, followed by a hail I could just distinguish as the vessels neared each other.

"Keep them until his lordship has time to look into the matter," said the voice faintly in the distance.

"Aye, aye, sir," bawled Mr. Rose.

"Hold on," I cried desperately, "tell him who we are and let us go ashore. This outrage has gone far enough"—

"Kape quiet, ye gentleman, or I'll be for

jabbing yez with me baynit," growled private Rooney, and he held the point against my ribs.

"It's no use," said Barron, smiling pleasantly, "we are in for some sport. It's a wonder, though, that his lordship didn't recognize me from that lieutenant's description "—

"Ef yez opin that ugly mug agin, afore the lootinant comes below, I'll cut off yer elephant years and jam them into it," said the soldier, Rooney. And then we kept quiet while the schooner drove steadily along up the river. Sometimes she tacked around the bends and sometimes she flew along with the wind fair, but before dark we knew by the sound of the rushing water, that could be distinctly heard through her sides, she had traveled many miles, and we were a long way from Judkins' Hall.

Just before coming to an anchor for the night the forecastle pivot-gun was fired at some hostile object, and there appeared to be some excitement on deck, but this soon subsided. Then the anchor chain roared through the hawse pipe and the sound of rushing water ceased. Men began to swarm below, and it was evident that the schooner had made her run for the day, and that unless Lord Dunmore interested himself quickly in our behalf we would spend the night uncomfortably.

It was late in the evening when the sergeant who had captured us came below. He made his way to where we lay through the crowd of sailors and soldiers who were sitting about talking and eating their evening meal, and looking at us.

"Th' Captin wishes to say a few whurds t' th' gentilman what stretched him out this day on th' main deck," he observed to the men guarding us. "'Twas a good stroke, sure, but the Captin av th' *Hound* keel-hauled two men, just lately, for trying to excite dishorder on th' beach, so it must be a hanging th' owld man is afther to-night. Bring thim right along wid ye, me sons."

Then he made his way on deck and we followed after him with a soldier at each elbow.

We went quickly aft, and just as I turned

to go down the cabin companionway I looked astern and saw the dark loom of the frigate's hull through the darkness. Then we filed below into the Captain's cabin. At the head of the cabin table sat Captain Cahill, and in front of him stood a flask of spirits. On either side, within easy reach, lay a pistol with the flint cocked back over the priming, and behind the Captain's chair stood Mr. Rose and two other officers. The Captain looked little the worse for the blow Will had given him, but his eyes shone fierce and green as a tiger's, as they met my cousin's look.

"Captain Cahill," said I, "for I believe that's your name, you will do yourself a favor if you set us ashore instantly. This outrage, sir, has gone far enough."

He turned his fierce little shifty eyes to me, but took no other notice of my words. He sat there, silent and grim, and slowly filled his glass from the bottle in front of him. Then he drank off the contents. As he drained the last drops with his head held backward, his eyes met mine squarely and his fury burned within him. He bit savagely through the glass tumbler and ground the splintered fragments between his teeth, and then spat them from his bleeding lips. Then he hurled the remainder of the tumbler to the deck with a crash, and sat there silently glaring like some fiend from hell. Finally he spoke.

"It is now nearly nine o'clock," he said slowly. "When three bells strike I shall drop all three of you overboard, and you shall have three twelve pound shot—one apiece—along with you. Lord Dunmore requests that you shall not be hurt. You will see, Mr. Rose," he went on, turning to his lieutenant, "that no violence is done these gentlemen. Do you understand, sir? Simply lower them carefully over the side with a shot fast to the right foot of each, and see that their hands are tied to prevent them from hurting any one. You may take them forward, sergeant.

We were on our way forward again and just on the point of entering the fore-hatch, when the sound of oars, working in oarlocks with a man-of-war's sweep, fell on our ears. The sergeant stopped and looked over the vessel's side.

"It's the Guvnor's boat," said one of the soldiers. "'E's comin' to pay his respects to the skipper, an 'e'll find 'im in a fine state for argyment."

"'Pon me sowl, it is," said the sergeant.

"Pete, you an' Rooney, here, take the folks below while I see to his ludship."

Before we reached the hatchway the boat was alongside and an officer climbed quickly on deck, where he was met by the sergeant.

"The Governor sends his compliments to Captain Cahill, and wishes him to send the prisoners he took to-day to the frigate for examination," said the officer, and as he spoke I recognized him as Captain Foy's under-lieutenant whom I had met several times before at Harrison's house.

I called to him before anyone could stop me, and the next instant we were shaking hands before the astonished soldiers.

"You have come in good time, Mr. Jones," I said, "and for Heaven's sake get us clear of this vessel and its lunatic skipper."

He laughed heartily as the sergeant came up and saluted. "This way, if ye plase," said that soldier, and he led him aft.

A few minutes later the sergeant came forward, accompanied by Mr. Jones of the *Fowey*, frigate, and we were ushered over the side just as the lookout, forward, struck off three bells.

"'Twas a narrer escape, me son," whispered the sergeant to Will as he went over the side. The next minute we were on our way to the frigate.

CHAPTER VI

"It's all very well for your lordship to laugh," said Will, an hour later, after we had been served with an excellent meal, washed down by delicious wine, at the Governor's cabin table, "but had you been busy with other matters to-night, we would have been comfortably buoyed in the mud at the bottom of the river."

"He is an uncommon rascal, that Cahill," laughed Dunmore, "but, my dear Byrd, you should not take arms against His Majesty's Governor, even in fun. Ha! ha! It would have been droll, 'pon my word, ha! ha! May the Lord roast me if it would not

have been a joke to have seen you tl ree
gentlemen buoyed in this most muddy
stream. It is a revelation, Byrd, a revelation, sir, from Providence. A sign of the
times and an omen for you to take advantage of without delay. It is an insight into
the future and should hurry you to take up
arms in His Majesty's just cause. Think of
it, if it had not been for his Majesty, the
King — as represented by myself — you
would have been at the bottom of the river
to-night to remain there, perhaps, through
all eternity ; for I take it that the angel
Gabriel would have to blow a mighty blast
to lift you out of this most sticky Virginia
soil."

"But if it hadn't been for His Majesty,

the King, as represented by that truculent skipper on the schooner over there, we might now be dining in the charming company of Miss Judkins and Miss Carter, to say nothing of the mistress of Judkins Hall," said Barron, smiling at Dunmore with a beaming face.

"And have lost the honor of dining with his excellency, the Governor," I put in hurriedly, for I thought I perceived an uncomfortable look gather on his lordship's countenance. The two officers present, Captains Foy and Graham, also began to look a trifle annoyed.

"But where are we, anyhow, Lord Dunmore?" asked Will. "Your excellency has rescued us, true enough, and made the matter all the better by adding this splendid dinner, but whereabouts on the river are we?"

"As near as I can judge, we are about twenty miles above Westover. Hey! Captain Foy? Isn't that about the reckoning?" replied Dunmore. "And if we have good luck and little fighting, we shall be through our business in this part of the river and on our way down stream before this time to-morrow evening. There is very little to do after all. Graham, here, and Fordyce of the *Hound* had some little difficulty yesterday with a small party of rebels, but they were all shot or dispersed except the leaders, who were keel-hauled by Captain Fordyce. He and Cahill are very able men in their line of work and their vessels are well adapted for these inland waters. But it is a very malodorous business and the sooner we get clear of these unhealthy swamp vapors, and get a sniff of salt air, the better. I hope, Foy, you will see that plenty of sulphur is burned aboard to-night."

"Can we be landed to-night?" I asked.

"Yes," said Will, "can we get ashore? They will expect us at the Hall and will be much troubled if we don't get back before bedtime."

"I don't see how it can be done, do you Foy?" said Dunmore, "We had an exchange of shots with the shore, as you may have noticed from the schooner, just before coming to anchor, and I would hardly think it wise to send a boat in there at this time of night. You wouldn't care to land there this evening, would you, Graham?"

"No, your excellency, it would hardly be safe, " replied that officer.

" Besides," continued Dunmore, "Fordyce stopped at Harrison's to take him and his party aboard the *Hound*, and from Fordyce's description of your affair on the beach with Cahill's men, they will probably be satisfied that you are in safe keeping for the night. Harrison was in a hurry to get to Norfolk, as he expected to sail for England soon,—so his note said—and I gave Fordyce orders to end his patrol there and start back immediately. He will go down on the morning tide and meet us below in a day or two. Cahill, and some of those small craft astern of us can finish up the work here and above us."

"Then we shall have to spend the night aboard?" I inquired.

"I am sorry to force my hospitality upon you, gentlemen," said Dunmore, "but I see no other way out of it. Anyhow, I take it for granted you would have joined us to-morrow, in the interest of the King, so the hardships will not be so very great. However, if you would rather go back aboard the *Black Eagle* and spend the evening with Captain Cahill, you may do so. Shall I call away the boat?" And as he said this his eyes twinkled with some little amusement,

"Give yourself no more trouble on my account, your excellency," said Barron, "I am, as you know, an old soldier and have no relatives to speak of. I find myself just as much at home in a strange bed, be it ever so comfortable, as in any other."

"Not a bad idea, Captain," answered Dunmore, "not a bad idea, sir; but before we think of turning in, Captain Foy and Graham here would not be adverse to open-ing a bottle or two more with you. Stew-ard! You may clear the table and bring some of that stuff captured yesterday. It may strike you as strange, gentlemen," he continued, "but that beggar who lives near Jamestown keeps most remarkable liquor. May the Lord pickle me, if it isn't equal to any I have ever tasted at home."

"And a most remarkable man he was, too," put in Captain Foy.

"He did show more or less nerve of a peculiar order," said Graham.

"How was that?" asked Will.

"Well, you see," said Captain Graham, "we went ashore on the island to reconnoitre, as we had heard of the large gathering at Williamsburg. The first thing that greeted us on landing was a couple of rifle shots. These appeared to come from the bushes near Jacquelin's house, and one of them struck poor Billings in the pit of the stomach and passed through him, poor fellow. We finally made a landing a little farther up stream, where there was more cover, and the first thing we encountered

on getting ashore was a motely crowd of
farmers, armed and ready to fight us.
There was one fellow, I believe they called
him 'Bullet,' who is a fierce rebel, and
another mounted on a powerful bay mare,
who rode with his left arm in a sling and had
a strangely attired negro servant to carry a
couple of rifles for him.   These were the
only dangerous men in the crowd, for the
rest had no organization and appeared to
obey no commander, so they quickly broke
and fled at the first fire.   Four of them
remained, however, and these two   have
just described were the ones who cut their
way through our men with their swords and
escaped.   The other two were captured, for
they refused either to run or cease fighting.

One was Jacquelin, who owns the house, and the other a man named Horn. Fordyce was coming up just then and I turned them over to him. He tried to get some information about Mr. Henry's mob out of both of them. Jacquelin had his fingers punched with a belt punch without so much as saying a word, and the fellow, Horn, was seated on a hot stove until the breeches and skin were burnt off his buttocks, but all he did during that time was to curse His Majesty most heartily. Fordyce started to keel-haul him, and had the line made fast to his hands passed under the schooner's bottom, but somehow the line fouled just as he was drawn under the bilge, and by the time they cleared it and pulled him

aboard again he was as dead as a mackerel.
After Jacquelin had his turn, he offered to
lead us to Williamsburg, or anywhere else
we wished to go, and the beggar told a yarn
about some good wine in his cellar the men
had failed to find.   We stopped at his house
again, and four of us went with him to find
the stuff.   He did have a door we had over-
looked and he showed it to us.   The cellar
was full of this stuff you see before you, and
while we stood at the entrance admiring the
flasks the rascal shoved all four suddenly
inside the door and banged it to and locked it.
Then he started across the island like a scared
rabbit.   That's the last anyone saw of him,
for, as usual in such cases, by the time the
men heard us and saw what had happened,

he was too far off to hit and there wasn't a man there who shot within a fathom of him."

"That must have been a very interesting affair," said Will, somewhat coldly, "but if you are through I would like to go to bed. I am a little fatigued from the day's excitement. No thanks! I do not care for any more wine. I hope your excellency will excuse me." And he rose from his chair.

Lord Dunmore looked sharply at Byrd, and appeared a trifle annoyed, but he said nothing.

It was easy to see that Will's sentiments were not exactly in accord with our hosts, and that a strained relationship would exist between them if something were not done quickly. It was evident that Lord Dunmore expected us to accompany him as loyal subjects on the morrow, and I knew it would need some keen acting on our part to enable us to avoid giving up our residence at the Hall and becoming refugees for an indefinite period. My heart was anything but light when I thought of Harrison, — with the ruffian Fordyce to back him,—having things his own way down the river. But as I only thought of Berk as a misguided gentleman, a little over-zealous in his duty to the King, the only trouble I anticipated was some obstacle I felt he would place in our way when he found we wished to remain at home. At all events, I knew I must not antagonize Dunmore, or he would fail to put us ashore

the next day as we hoped he would. Therefore I reached for poor Jacquelin's wine and
drank his excellency's health, and Barron
needed no urging to follow my example.

Will remained standing until I explained
that he was suffering from the shock of the
discharge from Cahill's pivot-gun, where-
upon the Governor was much amused and
laughed immoderately as I described how
the ball covered us with sand and gravel.
Then we finished the bottle, and after bid-
ding his excellency good night, the steward
ushered us into the officers' cabin where a
state-room had been made ready for us.

As soon as we were left alone, Will burst
forth into a perfect torrent of abuse against
Dunmore and his underlings. Barron and I

tried to stop him lest some one should hear the noise, but it was only after he had called them every villianous name he could think of that he at last consented to keep quiet. As for myself, I have said before that the Judkins family were not of a nervous or excitable disposition, and are not carried away by wild and insane thoughts of mistaken patriotism, but I had decided that evening that the King would soon have another enemy of my acquaintance. By the present state of the feelings of both Barron and Byrd, I thought it highly probable that there would be several more.

Will finally turned in and I did likewise, for we were very tired. Barron sat a long time apparently lost in thought, holding his half-removed boot in his hands. Then he spoke.

"Poor Horn," he muttered, "I owed him for two gallons of gin." And then he undressed and turned in without another word.

CHAPTER VII

The next morning the frigate was under way before we were up, but as the water appeared shoal at the end of the reach, she was anchored to await high tide, for the river is very narrow here and dangerous for a large vessel to turn about in. When we arose and came on deck a little later, we had the pleasure of seeing our friends, or rather enemies, of yesterday, pass close under the frigate's stern; and as they did so Barron leaned over the rail and saluted Captain Cahill very pleasantly and wished him a safe and happy voyage.

We stood on the *Fowey's* high poop and

watched the swift little schooner pass up the river and disappear around the bend above us. Soon afterwards we heard the rattle of musket firing, followed by the heavy, deep boom of her pivot-gun. After the reverberating echoes died away along the wooded shores, all was silent. The sun broke through the river mist and shone warmly on the muddy water, and the day promised to be bright and quiet. The two small craft that followed the schooner now took in their sails and put out their oars, and their niggers pulled to a lusty chorus.

Dunmore was up early. He was evidently annoyed at having to spend so much time on the river, for he came on deck in quite bad humor. He greeted us rather stiffly, and then turned to Captain Graham who had also just made his appearance.

"What is that firing about?" demanded the Governor in no uncertain tone.

"I don't know, your excellency," replied Graham.

"Captain Graham," said the Governor, "you will please tell me just what you know, sir, quickly. It won't take a minute, sir, or else write it down on a slip of paper. Send Mr. Johnson to me, sir!"

The Captain went forward on the poop, and a moment afterward a young officer appeared coming aft. He saluted the Governor and stood attention.

"Mr. Johnson, it is your watch on deck, sir. What was that going about on board the *Black Eagle?*" inquired Dunmore.

"I d-d-do not k-k-know,— your "—

"Call the Corporal of the guard, sir. Don't stand there and stammer at me, sir," cried the Governor, interrupting him and waxing furious.

The poor lieutenant retreated to the break of the poop, closely followed by his master, but he was too excited to speak plainly.

"Corp'ral g-g-g'ard! Corp'ral g-g-gard!" he cried weakly, but there was no response from the main deck.

"What are you doing, sir!" thundered Dunmore as he came up behind him.

"Trying t t-to c-c-call the Corporal of the g-g-g'ard, your "—

"For God's sake, Mr. Johnson call somebody. Call somebody, sir, quick," cried his lordship, walking to and fro across the deck and wringing his hands. Then, as he came to where the Lieutenant stood, he could stand it no longer and waxed into a frenzy.

"Do something! Call somebody! Do something for God's sake! Do something Mr. Johnson, or get off this ship," he cried. And the young officer, showing him self to be a man more fitted for action than words, dashed down the companion ladder and dragged the corporal he wished for up again by the collar of his coat.

Then, after much swearing and questioning, the Governor heard that Captain Cahill had fired upon a small hut, just visible beyond the bend of the river. I tell these events that happened on board the *Fowey*, frigate, to give an idea of the Governor's temper, and also because every incident of that time stands out clearly before me. Mr. Jones, the young officer who took us off the *Black Eagle* was very pleasant to us, and warned us against the tempers of Captain Foy and the Governor, after which he kept out of our way, and we saw him no more to speak to while we were aboard the ship. He was a promising young man and I hoped to have him help us get ashore, but he evidently thought it best not to be intimate with neutrals.

After breakfast his lordship was in better spirits, and these were more improved later in the morning upon the arrival of a small boat which carried Mr. Robinson, a noted tory, and several of his family to the frigate. Mrs. Robinson was a woman of fine presence, and her daughter might have been said to have been beautiful, judging from the standard of those days, but she was no longer young and her lack of success in the matrimonial field appeared to have soured her temper. These people were made comfortable in the officer's cabin and were very outspoken in their opinions regarding Mr. Patrick Henry.

When the tide turned in the afternoon and began to run a strong ebb, the frigate was gotten under way, and, with her working canvas set, headed down stream. The wind was so light that, in spite of the most careful steering, she was run on a mud bank before going much over a mile. Captain Foy, however, was equal to the occasion. He soon had a kedge out and before the falling tide left her fast he warped the ship back again into the channel. Bad luck did not desert us here, for the frigate had hardly gathered way again before she piled heavily upon a sand bar and all attempts to pull her off proved useless. It was then decided to await the next high water.

The day passed stupidly enough in spite of the presence of Miss Robinson on board. We were all anxious to get down river and Lord Dunmore was now in such a bad humor that he refused flatly, and with some energy, our request to have a small boat put us ashore, so we could walk the twenty miles or more across country to Judkins' Hall.

But we were not the only ones to suffer from his lordship's temper. Mr. Johnson, the young navigating lieutenant, came in for his share also.

He was standing on the edge, or break, of the poop, after the frigate had run hard and fast aground, and was much upset in his mind, although the accident was unavoidable.

A little imp of a powder-monkey boy thought to take advantage of a moment when his back was turned, to imitate his defect in speech and make faces at him for the benefit of the ship's company. The officer, however, turned and caught him in the act.

"Damn you, sir! Come to the m-m-mast!" he bawled, and Lord Dunmore, hearing the noise, came forward to see what was the matter, and take a hand in the disturbance if occasion demanded it.

"What has he done?" asked the Governor, as the boy came aft crying with fear.

"Nothin'," snuffled the little rascal, speaking before anyone could stop him. "'E just sez, 'Dam you, sir, come to the mast,' an' I comes."

"Did you swear at this boy for nothing?" demanded the Governor.

"No, your excellency," said Mr. Johnson. "I said d-d-damn y-y-you, sir, c-c-come here, because he"—

"That will do!" thundered the Governor. "Go to your quarters in arrest, sir. I won't have you swearing at my men for nothing. Go, sir!" And after this affair we gave his excellency a wide berth for the rest of the day.

The next morning the tide floated us clear, and we got under way just as the *Black Eagle* came around the bend above us. She soon caught up with the frigate and we learned that she had a dozen or more prominent tories aboard who wished to take refuge with the royal Governor.

We stopped twice on the way down the river, once to take aboard a tory named Thornton, who lived on a large plantation on the south side, and once we stayed an hour or more on a mud flat.

It was nearly sundown before the white

pillars of Judkins Hall showed through the fringe of willows on the river bank. The red light of the setting sun flooded the south portico and a pane of glass in a window, catching a ray at an angle, burned like a bright eye for an instant as we drifted past.

Dunmore reluctantly consented to send us ashore in a boat with Mr. Johnson and a guard of soldiers to see if anyone remained at the Hall, and if so, to help carry what luggage there was to be sent aboard the frigate. My slaves could follow us in the small craft. As the boat drew near the beach, where only a few days before Bullbeggor had won his strange victory over Harrison, we looked for some signs of wel-

come from our people.   Not a leaf stirred in
the calm of the bend, and not a sound from
the shore broke the ominous stillness of that
warm, clear evening.   None of us spoke
and even Barron's face appeared grave with
some thought of impending evil.   The sun
shone on the sweating faces of the rowers,
and the regular clank of their oars in the
row-locks beat time to my heart throbs as I
waited to learn what was wrong.

When the boat's keel struck the sand, we
sprang quickly ashore and proceeded rapidly
by the river path toward the Hall.   On entering the fringe of bushes and undergrowth
on the river bank I thought I heard a
strange noise close by me to the right.   We
stopped a moment and listened, but the four

men and Mr. Johnson, who were following close behind us, came up, and we started on again toward the Hall.

All of a sudden I heard a faint cry.

"Marse Dick!" it said feebly, and the voice came from the direction I had first heard the noise. Barron, Byrd and myself heard the cry simultaneously, and we instantly started toward the spot from whence it came. The next minute we broke through a thicket of blackberry bushes, and found a small cleared spot in the midst of the grass and briars.

There, lying upon his back, with his left hand held over a nasty cut in his abdomen, was my boy, Sam. The poor fellow saw me and I caught his glad look of recogni-

tion, but his glance wandered back of me
to Mr. Johnson and his men, and his look
turned to one of savage fury. He started
to rise, but I quickly held him in my arms
while the rest crowded around us.

"What's happened?" I gasped. "Where
is mother and Mary—and Miss Carter?"

"Miss Mary, she gone wid Marse Berk—
all alone—old missus and Miss Rose gone
away, too," said the poor fellow, with great
difficulty.

I looked at Will and saw him turn ashy
pale and his jaws set until the bands of
muscle in his lean face seemed about to
break with the strain.

"What rascal do you suppose did this?"
asked Mr. Johnson, coming up closer and

noticing the look on Will's face. But no one answered.

"Who gave you that cut, Sam ?" I asked, bending over him and gently removing his hand from the gash. "Get some water, quick !" I continued to the men, but Barron had already started for the boat, where he found a bailer, and returned in a moment with it full of water. In a few moments Sam felt better, and I immediately set to' work to dress his wound. "Who cut you ?' I asked again, for I saw he hesitated about telling me. I soon had a bandage in place, and then I repeated the question.

"Marse Berk," he finally whispered, and as he did so Will leaned over him to catch the words. "He an' that Captain were here—Marse Berk—he wanted Miss Mary to go off alone with him on the schooner—an' he took her—she wanted to wait for old missus an' she cried—I came—so he killed me."

"But mother and Miss Carter, Sam, quick; where are they ?" I asked, frantically.

"Dunno, Marse Dick. I'se been here sence yesterday—I ain't seen no one—they all must be gone somewheres, too."

"Carry him to the Hall," I said to the soldiers, and then Will and I started on a run towards the house. On reaching the front door we found it shut fast, but Will burst the fastening of a window on the verandah and sprang into the dining room, and I followed at his heels. I bawled out my mother's name, and Will cried out for my sister, but our voices echoed through an empty house. There was not even a slave there.

We quickly went through the rooms upstairs, and then through the pantries and kitchens in the rear, without finding a single house servant. Then we started for the slave quarters to see if anyone had remained there, but not even a single pickaninny was in sight. Everywhere there were traces of hurried preparations for departure. Clothes were scattered about the floors, and in the servants' dining room the evening meal lay untouched upon the table. We went outside and looked about the court, and then went to the stables. We had only been through the empty stalls on the lower floor, when we saw two of my niggers coming on a run through the field to the northward.   They had seen us and had come from hiding places, and in a few minutes they were with us and seizing our hands, thanking us for coming back again.   Then Mr. Johnson came up with his men, carrying Sam on a litter made of their crossed muskets, and Barron showed them the way to a couch in the slave quarters.

My two field hands, who were telling me what had happened, were ready to run at the sight of the soldiers, but I bade them be still and tell their story.

They told how the schooner, *Hound*, had anchored just off Harrison's plantation, the evening we were captured by Captain Cahill, and how Berkley Harrison had come over to the Hall with Captain Fordyce and a file of soldiers. Then all hands had gotten drunk, in spite of my mothers' presence, and Harrison had insisted on my family and Miss Carter accompanying him to Norfolk on the vessel. My mother had remonstrated at this high handed business, but Harrison stormed and threatened, and vowed he could not keep the soldiers from looting and burning the Hall if they were not all on board and ready to sail within an hour. My sister took him outside to try and get him into a more reasonable mood, and that was the last anyone on the plantation, except Sam, saw of her.

After waiting half an hour, my mother and Miss Carter became alarmed at her absence, and also at the actions of the soldiers, who began to fire their muskets at random. Upon looking for their Captain, they found him sitting on the verandah with a bottle of spirits on a table before him and much the worse for what he had already drank. He informed my mother roughly that Harrison and my sister had embarked aboard the *Hound*, which would sail within the hour. He then rose from the table and insulted Miss Carter, after which he staggered down to the shore and was carried aboard his vessel, leaving the Hall at the mercy of his men. These rascals broke into the women's side of the slave quarters and such a scene of riot

followed that my poor mother and Miss Rose
fled across the fields for their lives. They
reached Harrison's place and had the fright-
ened slaves, who were preparing to follow
their master, harness a horse for them.
Then they drove with all speed for Pendleton's Inn at the cross-roads several miles to
the eastward. Here they were made comfortable and were now awaiting news of
our whereabouts. As the men finished their
story, Barron reappeared with the Lieutenant, and I repeated some of the details.
Then I turned to the officer.

"You may give the Governor my compliments," I said, in a dry, rasping tone that
seemed to stick in my throat, "and tell him
that I am sorry not to be able to accompany

him to Norfolk this evening. I shall, however, hope to meet him and his party quite soon, and will make all haste after I see affairs attended to here. Mr. Byrd, and, perhaps, Mr. Barron, will go with you," and I gave Will a look that made him nod assent.

"I am v-very s-s-sorry, sir," stammered Mr. Johnson, "but the Governor's orders were positive. They were that all of you should return with me to the *Fowey*."

"Indeed ?" asked Will, blandly.

"And of course you will carry out the Governor's orders?" asked Barron, smiling pleasantly.

"At any cost, sir," replied Mr. Johnson.

"So you say," remarked Barron, still smiling.

"So I'll do," replied Mr. Johnson coloring a little at Barron's remark, "If you doubt me, sir, try me," and he looked about him for his men who now came straggling up.

"No offence, sir," put in Barron, quickly. "I merely repeated a remark said to have been made quite often in the society at court —a remark expressing doubt in the mind of the person making it, without reflecting in any manner upon the sincerity of the person telling of the supposed event."

"At any rate, you certainly will allow us time to collect my people and attend to my scattered property. Also, you will allow us to make what neccessary changes in our personal attire we see fit?" I asked.

"Certainly, sir," replied the officer, "the

frigate will anchor for the night in the broad reach a few miles below the bend, and you shall have plenty of time, not only to pack your effects, but to send for whatever relatives you wish to accompany you. The men, meanwhile, can collect your slaves and send them on ahead of us."

"We shall make our preparations," I answered shortly, and then I led the way into the Hall.

CHAPTER VIII

My first care was for my boy Sam, and after he had been properly cared for, he was carried aboard the small boat and made comfortable.

While we were changing our clothes, Will and I had a chance to discuss matters privately and decide what had best be done.

Knowing my sister's fondness for Berkley Harrison, I conceived the idea very readily that she had consented to go with him and marry him at the first convenient opportunity. Will declared that he would soon hear this consent expressed from her own lips, and that he would feel more relieved after hearing it. God alone knows what the poor fellow's thoughts were, and what hope still lingered within his breast. As for myself, my duty appeared now to lay first with my poor mother—and Miss Carter. My sister was off with the man she apparently loved, and nothing worse could happen to her than what had already occurred. I believed Harrison to be a gentleman and honorable in his dealings, although I did not agree with him in his political ideas and views.

Barron decided, positively, to accompany me and openly hinted that Williamsburg was the place he hoped to reach as soon as he helped me straighten out matters at the Hall.

"I will join you there also, as soon as I find my services are not needed at Norfolk," said Will.

"Then we will leave you here with Mr. Johnson," I said. "As soon as he gets tired of waiting for Barron and myself, you can go with him and join Dunmore, and meet us later with the forces under Colonel Henry."

While we were discussing our affairs, we were changing our shooting clothes for more suitable garments, and we were quite alone.

I took two silver mounted, Paris made pistols from a case, and concealed them carefully by sticking them in my belt under my outer coat. I may say here that these weapons were remarkable for their fine finish, and were the same I had used on one or two well known occasions before. They were the ones from which I had fired six bullets in succession, one day, upon the edge of a knife blade set twenty paces distant, and they could be relied upon. They had the advantage over most, for they exploded almost instantly from the flash of the flint.

After seeing to these, Barron and I then buckled on our swords; mine a fragile rapier which had formerly been part of the dress of a man of fashion, and his a more serviceable weapon, but still very light for field use.

"You will certainly allow me the privilege of escorting my own mother," I said to the Lieutenant, when we had finished our preparations and had come down stairs.

" Where is she?" he asked.

"At Pendleton's Inn, a few miles back in the country," I answered. "But, as I understand we are not exactly prisoners, you will have no objection to my going to her, and telling her of the arrival of his excellency, the Governor."

"Not only that, but you may take two men with you. There may be some of Mr. Henry's bush-fighters who might not be to your way of thinking, and who might dispute the way with you. Carry your sword if you wish. Is Captain Barron to accompany you? He may do so if you wish it, for, of course, I have your word that you will not stay any longer than necessary or go anywhere my men cannot go also without making trouble." Saying this he beckoned two stout soldiers aside and gave them some orders I did not quite hear.

I said nothing in reply to his remark about not staying, or leading his men into hostilities, for I wished to gain time, and I led the way quickly to the stables where saddles and bridles were procured.

The horses were at large, but in sight, grazing quietly in the pasture to the eastward of the quarters. My two field hands soon had four of them ready. Giving a nod to Barron, I leaped into the saddle, and he instantly followed my example. The soldiers started to mount in a more leisurely manner.

"Mr. Johnson," I said, turning quickly,

"I have not given my word as to not leaving you and your men. Mark that, sir. Therefore I bid you farewell."

The next instant I was loping gracefully down the carriage drive with that peculiar ease which you may have, perhaps, noticed as belonging to a Virginia country gentleman.

Barron's knee was rubbing against mine with each rise and fall, and the old soldier was smiling happily at the scenery lit up by the last rays of the setting sun.

I half expected to hear a warning bullet, and turned my head with my chin to my shoulder to see what was taking place behind.

Mr. Johnson waved his sword nervously

and shouted out something I could not understand, and then the two soldiers came galloping after us.

"We better avoid their company, for they are rough looking men," said Barron. "A soldier is good enough when properly commanded, but most unpleasant when in command. As for me, I intend to command some as soon as I can join the Major and the rest at Williamsburg."

"We must shake clear of these men before we get to the Inn," I said. "It would never do to have a dispute there before the ladies, although the advantage would lie with us. Suppose we slack up at the turn a mile above here and tell these fellows to go back. Perhaps Will will find himself kept pretty close when Dunmore knows we are not exactly in sympathy with the king."

"He will have tact enough to keep out of limbo, but I reckon Dunmore will try to make him take up arms against us," said Barron. "You spoke of a bend in the road; is that it ahead there?"

"Yes, but suppose these fools show fight?" I asked.

"That little side ornament of yours will do little good in that case, but I reckon I can hold them both in play. There was a time, if I remember rightly, when I knew something about the use of a sword—even a light one like this I have with me. When Braddock was down in the swamps I was a fair hand at pinning frogs. I reckon there isn't anything much better to eat than the reptile's legs, but I tired of them after the boys got me to eat the half raw legs of a skunk, by mistake, in the way of a joke. Most uncommon joke it was, but I certainly am right when I say I can taste those legs yet. Whoa! Steady, boys?" And we slowed our horses down to a walk.

The soldiers came galloping up, and the one who appeared to be a corporal, by the cheverons on the sleeves of his tunic, drew alongside of me and saluted.

"Sorry, sir, but orders are to accompany you to your party at the Inn and bring whatever luggage you wish to send back with me," said he.

"But I'm not coming back to the Hall for some time," I answered. "Do you wish to go with me to the militia camp? It's doubtful if they would receive you well, or allow you to return to the frigate after seeing your uniform."

"We only go three miles," said the man, "and if your party is not with us after traveling that distance, we will postpone meeting them this evening and shall return together."

"Shall is a big word," said Barron, laughing. "Don't you know any better than to use it to a gentleman? I reckon your discipline or early family training has been neglected."

"Our discipline aboard the *Fowey* is fair,"

answered the soldier, coolly, "and as for my family training, I don't think such things count for much. Family is nothing to me, for the only ones I ever knew of mine were cowardly and bad."

"Does that apply to your mother and father?" asked Barron, much amused.

"Most certainly. My mother was a woman on the streets, and my father was probably some chance acquaintance of a day or two, though I never heard his name, or have I ever met him; but if you think my ancestry makes me an inferior being to your self, I shall take pleasure in proving that a man's worth depends entirely on the educa- tion or training he gives himself, mentally or physically."

"You speak with great precision," laughed Barron, "and I am sorry not to have time to discuss your theory to a better advantage. That tall pine tree ahead, with the eagle's nest in its top, is a trifle over three miles from Judkins' Hall, so I regret to have to bid you good evening."

"If that really be so we shall all turn about here and go back to the boat. We shall proceed no further in this direction. I suppose you know I am master of arms on the frigate and quite capable of enforcing my words with this." And he whipped out a long shining sword and his silent mate did likewise.

"Of course you gentlemen will not resort to anything so vulgar and absurd as resistance. Therefore turn your horses and we may discuss other matters."

My temper had been steadily rising for some minutes past, and now it burst beyond my control.

I snatched out my rapier and dug my heels into my horse's ribs. The animal sprang forward twenty paces. Then I drew up and wheeled suddenly, and then bore down on that Corporal with all speed, my sword point aimed at his breast.

There was a crash as the animals and weapons met, and the next thing I knew I was lying on my back by the roadside, grasping the hilt of my puny, broken sword tightly in my right hand.

Barron sat quietly in his saddle and

laughed immoderately at me, while the soldier seized my horse by the bridle and bade me remount.

I sat up in the roadway a little dazed, but, collecting myself, I felt under my coat to see if my pistols were all right. They were there, so I arose, and, taking my horse from the Corporal, climbed painfully back into the saddle again. Barron then drew his weapon and slowly placed himself on guard.

"You may or may not be right in your theory, Mr. Soldier," said he, "but we are not to accompany you back to Dunmore. Mr. Judkins is a very young and inexperienced swordsman compared to yourself, but his mishap was due more to the worthlessness of his weapon than lack of skill."

"Tut! tut! I shall be forced to secure both of you with cords, if this nonsense proceeds any further," said the Corporal. "Put up your sword and waste no more time. Jim!" he called to his mate, "pass a line about Mr. Judkin's wrists, lest he continue this nonsense past supper time."

The soldier approached and bade me hold forth my hands that he might secure them with a line he produced from under his belt. I saw there was no use of putting off the crisis any longer, so I held out one of them—my right—and in it was gripped the butt of the straightest shooting pistol on the Virginia peninsula.

"Give me your sword hilt," I said, as I raised the barrel level with his eyes. But the fool had seen me unhorsed so grossly, that he laughed in my face, and made a pass at my weapon with his blade. I held fire while his point cut my cheek open, and I ordered him back, hoping I could spare his life. But he cursed me and pressed on, aiming a blow at my head to knock me from my horse, so I could wait no longer. Then, to save my life, I pulled down the flint. The next instant he lay dead in the road with a bullet hole in the center of his forehead.

It was all done so quickly that the Corporal and Barron sat looking on, hardly realizing what had happened. This gave me the moment I needed, so I pulled out my left hand weapon.

"Surrender your sword, sir," I cried to the Corporal, for the excitement of the fight was hot within me and my patience was at an end.

"Not to such a swordsman as you; it would disgrace me," replied the Corporal contemptuously, and he began the fight by making a pass at Barron, which the old Captain parried. Round and round and past each other went the horses, guided by trained hands, and the sword blades slipped with a ringing sound from lunge to parry. So fast did they fight that I found myself sitting there quietly in my saddle looking on, never thinking for an instant that one snap shot from my pistol would put an end to the affair. It was rapidly growing dark, but at that distance I could have broken the soldier's sword blade while it was in play, had I so wished.

The man was certainly a master of fence and I soon saw that Barron had no chance whatever with him. Still I never thought to fire upon a man engaged with another in a fair fight. The cut in my cheek bled freely, but I felt no pain or dizziness and was cool enough to think calmly. Once the thought came to me to get the dead man's sword and take part in the unequal affray, but I put it aside and made up my mind to shoot only at the last minute to save Barron's life. Suddenly a new idea flashed through my head and I instantly raised the pistol. The corporal's horse turned his nose in my direction and I marked the white blaze between his eyes.

"Crack!" And down both horse and rider went, just as Barron whirled a wicked cut at the soldier's head. The old Captain's weapon went wide and the Corporal jumped to his feet as lightly as a cat and was on guard again before Barron fully realized what had happened.

"Come!" I cried. "Let him go!" And I galloped away down the road before I finished speaking. Barron wheeled his horse to follow just as the soldier started for him. In an instant the animals were together, running neck and neck, with that Corporal within six feet of Barron's saddle, running as I had never seen a man run before.

Away we went, and for a second or two I was afraid Barron would be run through the back, but the pace proved a trifle too strong for our enemy.

Seeing this, the rascal made a vicious cut at Barron's mount and almost hamstrung him, and then he dropped back while the poor animal hobbled ahead desperately for several minutes, and finally brought up dead lame.

"That man will certainly prove he is equal to both of us," said Barron, "and put at variance all laws of heredity, if we don't do something to stop him."

"It's a pity I didn't shoot him, for that was my last shot," I said. "Here he comes, and unless you can hold him in check until

I get a charge into this pistol, we will indeed see Dunmore or the devil to-night."

As I spoke the figure of the Corporal showed through the gathering darkness, coming along the edge of the road at a smart walk with his long sword in front of him.

" You ride on ahead and let me settle with him," said Barron, quietly.

" It is uncommon shameful to have to run from this vermin," I said, "but I had him at my mercy once and let him go."

" So had he you, my boy," laughed Barron.

It did seem hard to have to get away from this creature, the acknowledged offspring of a prostitute, but it was apparently certain death to face him. I strove to get a charge into one of my pistols, but by the time I had the powder in the barrel he was up with us. He saw what I was about and instantly started for me. And then, yes, I shall have to confess it, then I put spurs to my mount and went down that dark road as though thirty devils were at my heels. The corporal's long sword could not reach me, so he soon gave up the chase and turned his attention to Barron.

In another minute my pistol was loaded and I was riding back again as fast as I could.

Barron had dismounted and they had just begun a passage as I rode up.

I was almost beside myself with rage and

I rode close to the soldier to be certain of my aim. I meant to end matters and would run no risk at night, so I shot quick and sure for the centre of the man's body and had the satisfaction of seeing him double up and drop in the roadway.

Barron stooped over him and picked up his long straight sword. He looked at it fos a moment and then passed it to me. It war a very heavy weapon and as sharp as a razor.

"Come," said Barron, "let us carry him into the bushes and go ahead."

The form of the soldier moved slightly as he spoke.

"I thought you killed him," he continued, and he sprang forward with his sword drawn back for a final thrust.

"Hold on!" I cried, "he's dead unless made of iron," and I jumped down from my horse and bent over the fallen man just as he started to raise himself.

"His belt! Quick!" I cried, and I grasped him around the body with all my strength.

Before he fully realized what was taking place, we had his elbows lashed fast behind him and I had a chance to find out why he not was dead.

My bullet had struck him just below the breast bone and over the heart, but between him and it was the cross belt buckle-plate of his uniform. The lead had flattened on this, but the stroke of the ball had sent him to the ground unable to move for over a minute.

"You are a most disputatious man, Mr Soldier," said Barron, good humoredly, "and at one time you had nearly all the facts necessary to establish the truthfulness of your side of the argument. I hope you are now convinced of the value of good breeding, and will not, in the future, thrust yourself into company uncongenial to your taste. However, you shall now accompany us to the Inn, for I would hardly trust you to return to Mr Johnson alone to-night."

"Had I believed you were not too scared to return," said the soldier, looking straight at me, "I would have followed you and killed you. Your horse is a good runner."

"And for such an absurd mistake, I very nearly killed you," I answered. "Had I known you were so bent upon mischief, I would have sent your soul to the devil some twenty minutes ago. We will now go back and get your mate's horse and you will walk between us the rest of the way."

In a few minutes we were back to where the dead soldier lay and Barron was soon mounted upon his animal—which, by the way, was mine, as were also the other three, and it caused me some little regret to lose two of them on account of this hard headed soldier.

We carried the dead man to the roadside and laid him in bushes. Then we proceeded quietly upon our way, and the moon rose like a huge ball of silver to light up the dark road.

CHAPTER IX

Pendleton's Inn, as you may remember, was a famous place in its time. Colonel George Washington often stopped there, and Mr. Patrick Henry often held a group of listeners spellbound with his peculiar eloquence on its wide verandah.

So proud was the proprietor of his distinguished guests, that the bed Colonel Washington usually slept in, and even a certain chair at the head of the dining room table, in which it was claimed he generally sat, have been preserved and pointed out to new-comers as objects of peculiar interest.

As for me, I have been to hardly a single

house between New York and Richmond
that has not boasted of possessing some of
the Washington furniture, and I have been
somewhat sociable in my habits.

Pendleton himself was a sad rake. But
his hospitality was known to the young
men for miles around, and his house was
often used as a meeting place on Sunday
afternoons, when the gentlemen would indulge themselves in such exciting sports as
cock-fighting and rat killing. Sometimes
affrays of a more sanguinary nature occurred within the limits of its broad orchard,
but these happened seldom, and, on the
whole, the Inn was considered respectable
enough for any lady in the commonwealth.

"I could not have stood it much longer,

my dear Richard," said my mother, the morning after our arrival. "I am too old for such scenes as that which happened at the Hall. I have not slept since Mary was taken away, and I have not had my bath for two days. All the servants ran away from that odious Captain and his terrible men. The only ones I have with me here are old Mammy Liza and Mary Jane Johnson. They were so old the men took no notice of them, so they hobbled all the way over here to me. But they cannot do anything, let alone fix my bath. And poor Rose, she has been so quiet. Not a word has passed her lips and she walks to and fro in her room with her head held tightly in her hands. The shock to her young nerves

at seeing such revelry has completely un-
strung her. Mammy Liza said she had
delirium last night, for she heard Rose
scream 'villain' and 'scoundrel' at the top
of her voice, and when she looked into her
room she was sitting in bed with her hands
clenched and her eyes staring into va-
cancy."

"I suppose she will not breakfast with us,
then," I said.

"I doubt it, but when I tell her you and
Captain Barron are to take us to Williamsburg, she may make her appearance in
time. You will not leave before we get
some news of Will and Lord Dunmore, will
you?"

"Possibly not," I answered, "but it is

hardly worth while to stay here. It is not likely the Governor will send a party this far inland after us, and as for Will, he will have no message of importance, even if he has a chance to send one. The Governor is in a hurry to get out of the river, for the climate does not agree with him. He is probably now as far down as Jamestown on his way out."

While I was speaking, Barron made his appearance, accompained by old Pendleton and half a score of armed men who had camped in the barn over night. These militiamen were on their way to join the forces under Colonel Henry, and they were armed and dressed in the most fantastic manner. They had just visited our prisoner, the Corporal, who was confined in a box-stall in the stable, and were in high good humor at the soldier's fierce threats and wild vaporings. Barron left these men on the far end of the verandah and came up and saluted my mother.

"I shall wait upon you, madam," he said, "just as soon as I ride over to my lodgings at the Widow Brown's house and attend to some little private matters there. It is not likely I will be back this way before next year, and I reckon I had better tell my landlady so. I think, however, that the Governor has made his last trip up the river, and, if that is the case, you can soon go back and remain unmolested at the Hall. But here comes our host, and he looks as if he had some matters of importance to communicate."

"Matam ees sarved wid her bickfust," spoke up old Pendleton, giving my mother a sweeping bow as he approached.

"In that case we will all go in together and fortify ourselves for the coming ride," I said, and I led the way to the table with my mother on my arm. We no sooner sat down than Miss Carter made her appearance. It was so late the night before when we arrived that I had not had a chance for more than a word of greeting with her, so she received Barron and myself very graciously.

In spite of her pleasant manner, I noticed the large blue eyes—I had seen only to admire so often before—were swollen and red, and the poor girl appeared to have suffered much. A man must be very selfish when in love, for it was quite plain to me that she was suffering more than I, yet I would not have had Harrison back there at that moment, had I been certain of his conventional behavior with my sister Mary. There is no use of denying it, I felt almost glad that he had run off with my sister. I was sure Mary loved him, and I reasoned that no harm could happen to her. I was equally certain Byrd would soon reappear with the news that she and Harrison were happily married. I was furious to see this beautiful woman breaking her heart for another, but was glad that his act was irrevocable and left the field clear for myself.

Barron waxed especially lively during the meal and ordered some of Pendleton's new cider, suggesting that Miss Carter and my mother drink some to refresh themselves for lack of sleep.

"It is weak enough, I reckon," said he, "for I call to mind the time Bullbeggor and I stopped here last year. His nigger, Snake in the Grass, had never seen this stuff, for the Major sticks pretty well to stronger waters. One cold night I gave the rascal a bottle filled with the stuff and told him to be careful with it, as it was very good. He sneaked off after supper into the woods and the Major couldn't find him again that evening. About midnight, while we sat smoking and talking, we heard a knock at the door.   I went into the entry and opened it, and there was Snake, shivering and shaking with cold.   'What's the matter, Snake?' I asked, when I got him inside.   'Oh, Marse Barron, yo' dun me mean,' he said, 'I went outen the woods to drink dat stuff on de quiet, an' I dun set thar fo' hours waitin fo' de drunk tu come—an' I'se nearly froze.   Yessah, yo' dun me mean, suh; sho' nuff mean, an' I'se nearly froze.'"

"Major Bull, he stopped here de oder day wid his nigger," added Pendleton.

"How about his shoulder, was it paining him much?" I asked.

"His shoulder! Nien it was a leedle hole, de pain shooded all through him. He has dem shooding pains always shooding through him. Dey was only leedle pains. Mein Gott! I never see de Major, but wid a leedle shooding pain."

"Then he went on and joined the militia at Williamsburg as he intended?" asked Miss Rose.

"Not only that," I put in, "but it was he who did some little fighting with that Captain Fordyce in the little skirmish below here the other day."

"And perhaps that is why the Captain acted as he did at the Hall. People are usually judged by the company they keep, and they all had heard of the duel," said Miss Rose, with a little sting of resentment in her voice.

"If that be really so, people's judgments

are most unjust, for a man certainly cannot always choose his own companions," I replied.

"I think he can," she answered.

"God grant that it be even so," I said, quietly, and I caught her eye for an instant.

Barron was laughing and looking at my mother, but Miss Carter appeared to take no notice of him and continued to eat her egg with more ill tempter than appetite.

When we were through the meal, Barron rode over to his lodgings and then returned within an hour. After that we had the horses brought up, and he and I acted as outriders to my mother and Miss Carter, who rode in Pendleton's chaise with old Mammy Liza and Mary Jane on the rear seat. One of

my field hands, who came over to the Inn,
acted as driver. Pendleton was to collect the
rest of my people and take care of them
until my mother was ready to return to the
Hall.

We started off with a contingent of the
militia bringing up behind us as a rear
guard, and among them walked the Corporal
with his belt strapped about his elbows behind him.

It was something uncommon in the way of
a procession, as we rode slowly down the
old Virginia turnpike. Barron, sitting his
horse in an easy, soldierly fashion, riding on
one side of the carriage, and I riding on the
other, while the motley men with muskets
and squirrel rifles, having the English cor-

poral in their midst, came straggling along through our thick yellow dust-cloud in the rear. The sun shone brightly and the birds sang merrily in the fields and woodlands, so our spirits rose, and even Miss Carter began to smile at Barron's jests.

The long, heavy sword I captured from the Corporal jangled uncomfortably from my belt, and it, together with my two silver mounted pistols, which I now carried in full view, gave me a most warlike appearance. But my clothing was of the latest fashion, and even my shoes showed the marks of care my poor boy Sam had bestowed upon them. But if I attracted some attention from the neighboring farmers, I hardly know what amount of interest was excited by the looks of our strange followers.

Some of these had their hair long and matted, hanging down over blouses or hunting shirts of deer skin, giving them an almost wild look. Their long rifles had the old fashioned heavy flint and wide primer and were of small calibre, best fitted for hunting squirrels and such game. But their powder horns held enough ammunition for a campaign, and they were all tolerable shots. Those who carried muskets appeared perfectly contented that their weapons made a loud noise and asked for nothing better than a range at which it would be almost impossible to miss an enemy—or hit a friend. Some carried old swords of the most unusual patterns,—looking as though they might have once done good duty as scythes,—and all carried knives. A young clown, from one of the upper counties, carried a musket with fixed bayonet and had the impudence to try and force the Corporal to put him through the manual of arms, even threatening to blow the soldier's head off if he gave an improper order. All of them were entirely without discipline, and all gave orders and offered suggestions at one and the same time. This, of course, invariably ended in a dispute that had to be settled by long arguments, in which all who wished to took part. Several times, during their bickerings, they fell far behind us, only to catch up again later on, and all day long their hilarious songs, accompanied by frequent fusilades of rifle shots, kept us in excellent knowledge of their whereabouts.

At noon we passed Doncastle's ordinary, where the affair of the gunpowder brought about the first distinct rupture between Lord Dunmore and the people. Everything appeared quiet and peaceful and the place showed no signs of war.

We had little conversation on the ride, and I found myself thinking a great deal of my poor boy Sam and Will Byrd. Will, I felt sure, would take care of the wounded fellow and endeavor to prevent him from falling into other hands, and I believed Sam would soon get over his hurt, for he was a powerful nigger, broad-built and with good pluck. I tried to imagine what would happen to Harrison if Sam ever met him before matters were peacefully settled. But then

I knew that Harrison would not return to his plantation until the war was over, and I believed it would be a long time before peace reigned again in the colonies.

At intervals during the ride I came close to the carriage and endeavored to engage Miss Carter's attention, but she appeared so sad and listless that, out of sheer pity, I forbore to worry her with my presence. Once I thought I noticed her looking at me intently with a curious, searching expression in her eyes for some moments, but when I turned my gaze in her direction she immediately stared vacantly at the scenery ahead.

I told my mother of my intention of joining the forces under Mr. Henry, and strange to say she did not appear to be either surprised or disappointed. On the contrary, she began instantly to give me all manner of advice about taking care of myself when camping in the field, and above all implored me never to expose myself to the danger of getting shot.

"It is absurd," said she, "that a gentleman should expose himself to the hurts which belong to the common, vulgar soldier. A true general always takes care of himself, for with him rests the care of the whole army. Should anything happen to the officer in command, what, oh what would become of those poor fellows dependent upon him for his high courage and intelligence? They would certainly be lost, and it is for them, my dear Richard, you should sacrifice all brute feelings of ferocious courage and keep yourself in hand."

Barron agreed with her in her sentiments, and she made him promise faithfully that he would never leave my side in the hour of danger, and never allow me to be carried away by my youthful ardor; all of which he did with a grave countenance, and some little ceremony, in spite of a little frivolity on my part.

In the late afternoon we caught sight of the white tents of the militia, and soon afterwards we were entering the quaint old town of Williamsburg. We headed for my uncle's house, which stood near the college, in the best part of the town, for my uncle's wife, Aunt Jane, as I called her, was a person of some prominence, and was of the ancient family of O'Brian, which, as you know, was once royal.

The streets were full of men from the surrounding country, who gathered in groups as we passed, and pointed at us and stared as though we were something remarkable. But they were all rough men, who had never seen much, and belonged to the outlying settlements and farms where no gentleman ever gets, except by hunting or some mishap. The men who appeared to be soldiers wore no regular uniform, and might have passed for a lot of armed yokels starting out on a coon hunt.

As we drew near our destination we

heard the sound of galloping horses, and presently several mounted men came riding around the corner ahead of us.

I recognized Patrick Henry and Colonel Woodford at a glance. The former had made himself a colonel of militia and rode a powerful grey horse at the front of the groups, while on either hand rode Colonel Woodford and Colonel Bullet. Behind them came several other gentlemen, well known along the James river for their anti-British politics. Among them I recognized Major Bullbeggor and also Mr. Jacquelin, who had been captured by Fordyce, and who had escaped from his captors by running while they were suddenly confined in his wine cellar. Still farther in the rear rode some mounted servants, with Snake in the Grass in their midst.

The Major saluted with a flourish as he rode past, as did the rest of the officers, and Snake's hat continued to rise and fall while his nodding, grinning face was turned towards us until the cavalcade disappeared in the direction of the encampment behind the college.

On arriving at our destination, we received a warm welcome from my aunt Jane and cousin Marion. Although my uncle, Thomas Burns, Esq., had died some years before, my aunt and cousin were living in the most comfortable circumstances. While they lived simply in their large mansion, they had an abundance of home comforts and many house servants, and cousin Marion, though only sixteen, was considered one of the wealthiest as well as prettiest women in Virginia. Aunt Jane was well known for her kind acts of charity and hospitality, so you may be sure there was nothing lacking for our comfort on our arrival at her house.

In spite of this Barron and I were all eagerness to go to the camp and report to Colonel Henry—as we now heard him called —for duty. Even the prospect of a few hours alone with Miss Carter and my pretty cousin Marion, was not enough to curb my impatience to be among the men, who I now felt certain would make some history to be handed down through all time.

I know Marion laughed at my warlike appearance, but I changed that a little by fixing my pistols under my coat and hitching up my heavy broadsword until it cocked up as prettily behind as a rapier.   In this attire I bade my pretty cousin good-bye, with cousinly privilege, and bowed low to Miss Carter. Then Barron and I mounted our horses and rode off with Marion's laugh ringing after us. She was a very pretty girl and as good as ever lived, but I thought very little about her as we rode down the main street in the direction of Colonel Henry's headquarters.

CHAPTER X

The first person we met on arriving in front of Colonel Henry's house was our old friend, Major Bullbeggor.

"I am feeling pretty peart, Mr. Judkins," he replied, in answer to my greeting. "That little punch Harrison gave me is almost well, and besides a slight twitching of the bones and some little stiffening of the joints, with a little pain shooting through them, I am feeling fine, sir. Yes, sir, feeling like a bird, sir. But where on earth did you get that English sword, and what brought you and your mother here so soon? Dunmore, for sure. No fear! The rascal passed down

the river this morning and I don't think he
will try coming up again. But what can
we do without ships or guns? We gave
them a dusting on the island, the other day,
and lost poor Jim Horn and three niggers
before leaving. Bullet and I had a hard
time to get out, and Snake took a slight
hurt."

"Yes, I heard all about it," I answered.
And then Barron and I told how we were
captured and taken aboard the vessels, and
how Harrison had served my people at the
Hall while we were absent.

The Major's eyes flashed as we told the
story and his hand went nervously to his
sword hilt. "I didn't hit him hard enough,"
he said fiercely, when we had told of the actions of the soldiers at the Hall.

While we continued speaking, we were interrupted by an uproar which arose from the street beyond the college, and on looking in that direction from which the sounds proceeded we suddenly saw the figure of a man, covered completely from head to foot with feathers, come running along the pavement towards us. Behind him came a howling mob, armed with every conceivable sort of weapon, and they pressed closely upon the runner's heels. The fugitive stopped suddenly in front of me and spoke out—

"If you'll give me that sword of mine for a few minutes, I think I might show these fools the absurdity of playing their infernal games upon one of his Majesty's soldiers," he said coolly, and I instantly recognized the voice of the corporal who had engaged us so hotly the day before. He was almost completely hidden under his coat of tar and feathers, and the only part of his face visible was his nose and eyes.

Barron and the Major burst into uncontrollable laughter, in which I joined.

But the man's tormentors were upon him before I had even time to consider his proposition. They surrounded him and began prodding him with sticks and bayonets, shouting and jeering in derision.

Bullbeggor was the first of us to recover himself. He drew his sword and struck his spurs into his powerful mare, making her spring forward through the crowd. He knocked down several men in his path and reined up alongside the prisoner.

"Disperse!" he roared.   "Break away!"
And he struck some of the men nearest him
with the flat side of his blade.   Barron and
I spurred forward and joined him, for the
natives were waxing furious at this inter-
ruption and I noticed one man bringing his
musket to his shoulder.   The Major saw the
fellow in time to avert disaster, and he
leaned forward and smote the weapon so
strongly that it fell from the scoundrel's
hands.   Then we closed around the prisoner
with our swords sweeping at arm's length,
and the Major thundered forth orders for
the men to disperse, threatening them with
all sorts of military punishments if they did
not.

But these wild men had no idea of discipline, and **feared** nothing, so they still crowded **sulkily** around us, brandishing their weapons and cursing us heartily for interfering with their sport.

The uproar had been heard at headquarters, and Colonel Henry appeared on the verandah accompanied by Colonel Bullet, Woodford, and some other officers. Colonel Woodford roared out orders, and some of the men about us turned to see who our new ally was. Then they suddenly recognized Patrick Henry, as he stood there in his waistcoat on the verandah.

There was something in the calm dignity of Colonel Henry's manner that arrested all the fierceness of these rough men's passions and drew attention to him as the magnet draws soft iron. He stood there on the verandah and held out his hand over that wild mob, and spoke, and in less than half a minute every man was silent and listening.

I cannot recall the words that fell from the lips of that grand orator, and when I think of him standing there speaking, it seems to me it was not the words at all that affected me, but the deep power of the man's nature.

I have heard men speak to men in my time, and have listened to some of the eloquent words of those who have made history; but nothing I ever heard compared to the power and force of those words that fell from the lips of that plain and uncouth officer standing there on the verandah of that house in Williamsburg.

He spoke to that mob of honor and manhood, and of the grand things of war, and bade them remember that mercy to a fallen enemy showed the difference between a coward and a man.

When he finished there was not one of that ruffian crowd who looked squarely at his neighbor, and two minutes afterwards there were not six of them in sight.

The only person there who appeared in no way affected by Patrick Henry's remarkable eloquence, was the English corporal.

He looked carelessly about him for a moment and then at Major Bullbeggor.

"I have to thank you," said he," for interfering with those farmers, for as you see, I am entirely unarmed and undressed—except for this growth of feathers. But I am no chicken sir, in spite of them. No, sir, I'm hardly classed as a chicken—as these two gentlemen with you might testify.

"If the ugly old duck, there,"—and he pointed to Barron—" would like to continue the argument we were engaged in last night, I think I might persuade him of the fallacy of his ideas concerning his birth and self importance."

"You have most remarkable powers of logic," laughed Barron, "and if reason and sword-play were analogous I doubt not that you could sustain your premise. But there are too many men like you in this world who wish to maintain their point by reason of false analogy. Therefore, I warn you that unless you mend your speech I shall turn you over again to Colonel Gibson's lambs, and they will hardly let you off so easily the next time."

"If they are his lambs," replied the soldier, turning and looking at Colonel Henry, "I take it he is a preacher, and now I mark it, the fellow has a most ecclesiastical mode of speech. One would think him an itinerant minister, holding forth to his flock of"—

"Silence! you dog," growled the Major, "know your betters, or I'll stretch you on the wheel." Then he beckoned to an orderly who stood nigh the steps of the house and in a moment the Corporal was led away to be scraped and scrubbed.

Barron and myself were then introduced

to Colonel Henry, Woodford, and other
officers in the group, after which we were
left to ourselves to discuss more or less
learnedly the probable outcome of affairs in
the colonies, while the older men went back
to their duties. I knew little or nothing
about military organization, so when the
talk drifted into certain channels I with-
held my speech. Before we left, however,
Barron and I had been assigned volunteer
positions; he as captain of a company of
farmers, and I as a lieutenant in it, all
under the command of Major Bullbeggor,
who, in turn, belonged to Colonel Bullet's
regiment. Rank was a pretty hard thing
to determine in those days, for nearly everybody was addressed as "Colonel" or "Major,"

no matter what they were in reality. Besides this, there were several jealous men in the Richmond assembly who pretended to doubt Colonel Henry's military ability, and for a long time I believed Colonel Woodford in command.

The brave and gallant Bullet, however, took the place assigned him without a word, as did Bullbeggor, Barron and myself, and we strove to get some discipline into the hunters and farmers who made up our rank and file.

Gibson's Lambs, as his command of wild men were called, were almost beyond the reach of discipline, and were little better than Indians, so at one time Colonel Woodford was strongly tempted to disband the whole outfit, but later on they began to show signs of intelligence and were kept in ranks.

We drilled and drilled, day after day, until finally we had the satisfaction of heading a poorly armed, but fairly well organized, set of men.

During this period we had several times had news of Berkley Harrison. He and my sister were apparently married and living happily together at Norfolk, but strange to say not a letter or word came direct from either of them. Of Will Byrd and Sam there had been no trace since they went aboard the frigate the evening I left the Hall. Barron sent several messengers to Norfolk to find out their whereabouts, but to no purpose.

Whenever I had time to spare from the camp, I usually came over to see my mother and cousin Marion. Miss Carter had seldom put in appearance until the day Snake in the Grass brought the news of Harrison and my sister living so happily together. Then her manner toward me instantly changed, and instead of being out of sight she always put in appearance whenever I called at my aunt's house, This amused me not a little, but I was not ready to indulge her whims too quickly, so I put off matters until I finally became so entangled with my pretty cousin that I was on the point of doing something foolish. But sometimes unforseen incidents happen that pull a man out of a drifting current.

One evening my cousin was not feeling well, so Miss Carter and I took a long walk around the encampment and visited Lord Dunmore's deserted palace. As we walked along the sound of a nigger singing arrested our attention. It was Snake's voice, and his deep bass notes rang weirdly through the gathering darkness. Snake had a strange habit of fitting all his feelings into song, and now he sang in deep mournful notes

"Dere is trouble ober heah
An' dere's trouble ober dar-r
An' I really do believe dere's trouble everywhar-r
Trouble, troub–ll
Trouble, troub–ll
Oh dere's trouble on de ol' man's mine."

We tried to stop him as he rode past us, but he pretended not to see or hear us, and rode away in the direction of the Major's quarters.

"Snake has a sorrowful mood upon him this evening," said Miss Carter, after the singing had died away in the distance.

"And by the same token, I reckon, there's some bad news ahead," I answered, "and we might as well go to the Major's and find it out."

When we reached there, we found that orders had just come for us to move to Norfolk and take part in the operations against the British. I was glad the news was no worse, and I must say I felt a great relief, in spite of those I must leave behind me.

This was my last evening to spend with my people, and I determined to know my fate in a certain direction, so I recalled a few things to Miss Carter that had passed between us.

"My dear Dick," she said, "you have a most charming cousin. Why don't you marry her?"

"In the first place, she would not marry me; and in the second, she is hardly to my way of thinking," I replied.

"But you might alter your thoughts and ask her; she is pretty, wealthy, and a lady born," said Miss Carter.

"So was your grandmother," I replied, "but that fact does not presuppose any love for her on my part, charming as she still is. You also have the qualities you have just mentioned, and you, you only, do I, or can I ever love."

"If that is so, I shall be blessed with a most stupid husband," said Rose—and that

was all. I bade her good-night at my
aunt's front door and I think, or rather
hope, it was quite dark. Then I went on
my way whistling, as happy as a boy.

The days that followed in the mud and
rain near Norfolk, were disheartening
enough, but I never for an instant de-
spaired. My whole life seemed filled with a
great coming joy, and even old soldiers like
Barron and Bullbeggor wondered at my
never-failing spirits. There were nearly a
thousand of us, badly armed and half-frozen
men, under the command of Colonel Woodford, camped at the end of the causeway
known as Great Bridge. It was December,
and the weaker men fell away rapidly, until
there were scarcely two hundred able rifle-

men left in the trenches on the night of the eighth.

I was lying in my tent on this night, listening to the rain and thinking happy thoughts of the joys in store for me when I should return to the Hall and marry the beautiful girl I loved. Barron slept with me and was snoring away at a great rate for it was long past midnight. I had just made up my mind to cease building air-castles and follow his example, and had fastened the tent flies and stretched myself out comfortably in my wet blanket, when a noise outside startled me.

It sounded like the stealthy tread of some-one bent on a secret purpose, which, at this hour and place, would probably be anything but good.

I reached carefully for my pistol and noiselessly cocked back the flint, and then stared through the inky darkness toward the tent fly. I lay listening for a moment or two longer and then was aware of something moving under the canvas at my side. In an instant I clapped the muzzle of my pistol to it and called out, "Stop!"

"For God's sake, take your pistol away and let me in, quick!" said a well known voice, and the next instant Will Byrd was inside the tent. Another form followed his and for a moment I was almost smothered by Sam's embrace.

"What time is it?" asked Will, quickly.

"Not quite three, I believe," I answered. "But for heaven's sake, how did you get"—

"Hurry, then, we have just about time," interrupted Will, paying no attention to my question. "They attack you at daylight. We have just escaped, and came through the swamp to avoid being taken by these farmers and held until too late "—

"Hello! What's the matter? Who's that?" cried Barron, starting up from his blanket.

"Will and Sam," I said, "They've just come over. The grenadier company from the fort will be on the causeway in an hour," And in less than a minute all of us were on our way to Colonel Woodford's tent to tell him the news.

Little noise was made as we gathered our men at the end of the causeway, and as we hurried about Will told me, between breaths that my sister Mary and Harrison were living in the town of Norfolk where Will had been held close prisoner until an hour or two before. He had failed to gain the good will of the governor on going back to the frigate after our flight, and both he and Sam were closely confined. As soon as Sam was able to work, he was taken out and sent, with a lot of other captured slaves, to help strengthen the fortifications of the town.

Here he heard the news of the proposed attack and managed to liberate Will and escape with him in time to warn us.

"When was Mary married, and at what church?" I asked breathlessly.

But Will suddenly turned away and did not answer and, taking an old musket from a farmer, pretended to be busily engaged in fixing the flint.

I was working hard with my men, trying to get an old twelve pounder into position to sweep the bridge, but the wheels of its carriage were so rotten and stuck so deeply in the mud, that they finally broke down completely, leaving the gun useless.

As the gray dawn of the winter morning deepened, objects began to grow more distinct. We shivered in our wet clothes and strained our eyes in the direction of the fort that covered the farthest approach to Great Bridge.

Something moved in the dim distance.

Slowly and surely it drew nearer, and then we saw the head of the British column coming silently over the long causeway.

I shook from head to foot with cold and excitement, and was so ashamed because I did so, I felt like doing something foolish to prove my courage. It was very trying to stand there on that cold, wet morning and not even speak above a whisper, or move more than a foot or two, while that column, with a company of grenadiers in the van, made its way to within speaking distance of us.

The enemy was so close that, even in that bad light, the features of the men were easily distinguished, and their hard, bronzed faces looked strangely fierce from under their tall grenadier hats. Then a nervous rifleman on my left blazed off his priming, and the next instant a hundred rifles rang out from the breastworks into a deep, rolling roar.

The head of the column seemed to melt away like an icicle in the sunshine. Men pitched over each other in a tangled heap of guns, arms and legs. But the rest behind them came steadily onward, firing together in volleys that sounded like a single report.

Our line fairly flamed with rifle flashes, and the men yelled and shouted at each dis- charge, until the blending of yells and mus- ket firing became almost deafening.

Suddenly the column wavered. Then backward it went and appeared almost on the point of breaking. Officers waved their swords and shouted furiously at the men, and like the gallant soldiers they were, they closed up and came onward again with a scorching fire that seemed to fairly fill the air with flying lead.

A bullet cut the coon-skin cap from the head of an old hunter at my elbow, but he never even winced, and coolly bit the end off his cartridge and rammed the lead home as if making ready to fire at a target.

They were within twenty paces of us now, and I fired my pistols with the certain knowledge that the bullets would strike within an inch of the spot at which I aimed. The officer leading the grenadiers sprang forward upon the breastwork, gave a shout to his men, and then, waving his sword, he brought it down with a sweep at my head. He was a brave fellow, and I did not know it was Fordyce until after my pistol bullet had passed through his body and he had rolled back among his men.

It was now almost hand to hand fighting, and the hot blasts of the muskets, firing in our faces, scorched the skin and blinded us so that nothing could be seen a few feet distant, but we had the advantage of only having to expose our faces, whereas the enemy had to stand to it in full view.

I saw Colonel Woodford ride past the line within a foot of me, sitting his horse easily in full view of the enemy, but he remained untouched.

The fight raged fiercely, but our men refused to be dislodged. The grenadiers were forced backward on the causeway, where they rallied upon the tory infantry coming to their support, and in a moment the smoke cleared away enough to see them forming for another desperate charge.

Again and again did they storm that line of riflemen, and each time they were repulsed and forced onto the causeway. Then, with great precision, they closed up and drew away, firing steadily as they went, the tory infantry leading.

A great shout went up from our victorious soldiers, and Colonel Bullet leaped, sword in hand, over the breastworks and called for the men to follow him. Bullbeggor pushed forward on the right, and led half a score of men onto the causeway, but the British fired so steadily, and kept their formation so well, that Colonel Woodford would not risk any mishap to mar so grand a victory. The men were recalled, in spite of the gallant Bullet's protests, but the rifle fire was kept up from the breastwork until the enemy was well across and out of range. All along the line of that long causeway they dropped from the ranks before the murderous fire of those Virginians, and when they at last gained the protection of the guns of their fort on the other side, there was not one grenadier left unhit. The rest of them broke and became a disorganized mob, making for shelter where it could be found, while the way now being clear the fort opened a heavy fire that soon kept our men under cover.

When I had time to look about me I was astonished at the small number of our wounded. In that hot fire it seemed to me that nearly everyone must get hit. But the poor light and breastworks had saved us many lives, and our victory was not robbed of its joy by the presence of many dead and wounded comrades. Not over a score of our men were hit, and only a few of these casualties resulted fatally. Barron had his coat cut in three places by balls, for he had exposed himself unnecessarily, and Bullbeggor had lost his hat and was bleeding from a scratch on his forehead where a grenadier had made a pass at him with his bayonet and then fired. The steel had cut the skin, but the bullet had missed and the discharge had blackened the Major's face until it was the color of his servant's. Snake wished to attend his master, but the Major waved him back and insisted on taking no notice of his hurt. He stalked up and down the line of men, with his drawn sword held before him, stopping now and then to see that a rifle was properly primed, or that the men did not flinch too much from the artillery fire and become disorganized in case of a renewal of the attack.

Finally the fire of the fort slacked up, and then ceased altogether, and we were able to go about unmolested. Twenty dead grenadiers lay piled up at our end of the causeway, their red coats stained with blood and dirt. Then, as the fever of the fight died away in our veins, we looked out upon those silent corpses and began to realize the grim glory of war.   Will joined me then and we shook hands silently over our success, and afterwards we started to do what we could for our wounded men.

CHAPTER XI

Shortly after the battle of Great Bridge the British evacuated Norfolk, and we followed hard upon their heels. Will and I happened to be together in the company that first entered the town, and we had some hot skirmishing before we got well into the streets.

He had told me little in regard to Harrison and my sister, but his sad face and silent manner spoke plainer than words the thoughts which were uppermost in his mind. Since the morning he crawled into my tent I had refrained from asking any more questions.

(246)

We had become separated from our men in a smart rally about a tory house, whose inhabitants had fired upon us and then fled, but Will continued to lead the way rapidly through the main streets toward that portion of the city where resided the most prominent followers of Lord Dunmore.

Even as we appeared in the streets people fled towards the water front, where the boats of the men of war were plying back and forth, taking the fugitives aboard in great numbers. Suddenly Will stopped at a corner and looked sharply across the street at a house whose closed blinds gave it a deserted appearance.

Almost instantly the front door opened and Berkley Harrison walked out. He saw us and turned towards us for an instant; then bowing politely he made his way down the street.

"Stop! Hold on!" I cried, and I ran across to intercept him. "Wait a moment, you have something to tell me," I continued as I caught up with him.

For answer he drew his sword and stood on guard. Will stood silently watching us.

"Hold on!" I cried. "Where is Mary? What do you mean by that?" and I pointed to his drawn weapon.

"Miss Judkins is upstairs," he said coldly, and he drew himself up to his full height, while that scornful smile I knew so well curled his lips. "If you wish to see her," he continued, "you will probably find her at home."

"But, Berk," I cried, "tell me, are you married, and is she going with you? It's but a step to the frigate's boat and our men will not come much closer. Tell me all about it, and h ow you intend to care for my sister?"

"You will have to excuse me, Mr. Judkins," said he. "I am not afraid of your men, but every loyal man has left this town, and I must catch the last boat to the frigate, where I have business of importance to attend to."

Then I realized the horrible truth that had begun to gain upon me since I noticed Will's suspicious lack of knowledge of Harrison's affairs. I was satisfied that Will had heard the true rumor of the affair, while he was confined in prison, and now my wrath swelled beyond my control and burst forth.

"You damned villian," I said, almost in a whisper, and I had my sword before me.

We went at it; I with my blood afire, he with the coolness of a born villain, who neither feared nor cared for anything.

The rasping ring of sliding steel and the noise of our shuffling feet were heard in the room above us, for in a moment a shutter clanged open against the wall, and I heard my sister's voice shriek in dismay.

I turned my head partially to try and see her face and slipped on the wet pavement. Then I felt something like a bar of hot iron passing through me and Harrison's cold, villainous face was close to mine. There was a sickening catching of the breath, but I sat my teeth hard as the scoundrel withdrew his weapon. Then I reeled and fell to the pavement.

But I would not go, quite. Everything seemed to whirl around me, but I drew my right hand pistol and cocked back the flint with fast weakening fingers. Harrison appeared in a fog, and to be going up a steep hill close to me, and then suddenly to be descending a frightful declivity as I raised my weapon slowly. The pavement seemed to heave upward again, and I marked the look on his craven features — for he knew what he was facing — and I pulled the trigger with the sight on his heart.

At that instant something struck the

weapon from my hand, and I was aware of Will Byrd standing over me with his sword outstretched.

I was going fast, but I drew my left pistol. Harrison was still standing near me, but appeared to be double. I fired into him but an object seemed to pass between us and something fell heavily to the pavement.

Then I thought I saw the villain sheath his sword and bow to me, with that same sneering smile on his face, and pass away out of sight down the long street. I tried to raise myself to follow him and got to my knees, then I pitched forward—

It was late in the evening when I regained consciousness, and found myself lying on a cot in a house which appeared to be an improvised hospital, as there were many wounded men about me. A wet compress lay upon my chest and each breath I took caused me sharp pain. I looked at the cot next to mine and noticed a familiar figure reclining there, and as I did so it sat up. Then I recognized Will Byrd, but could not tell how either he or I came to be where we were.

He saw my eyes open, and gazed sadly and thoughtfully at me; then he spoke.

"How is it Dick, do you feel better?" he asked.

"Yes," I whispered, "are you hurt too?"

"No, why?"

"What are you lying there for?" Then I suddenly remembered. "Where's Harrison?" I asked faintly, as the affair came back to me.

Will looked thoughtfully at me without speaking, and the expression of deep sadness came over his face again.

"Where is he?" I whispered.

" His body was thrown into a trench with some others outside the town," answered Will.

"Then you killed him? Or was it a dream, what?" I gasped.

"Don't try to talk, Dick. You remember you shot him, don't you? hit him through the body. I knocked your first pistol away, for your sister's sake, but you fired again before I could stop you. Don't talk any more and you will come out all right.

"There's not much dream about the whole business, I only wish there was."

CHAPTER XII

The evacuation of Norfolk by the British practically ended the war for a time in Virginia, and Dunmore soon sailed away never to return.

In a couple of weeks I was on my feet again, very little the worse for the wound Harrison had given me.

Will had been with me all the time and Barron and the Major spent nearly all their spare hours in the hospital.

The companies had now begun to disband, that is all except those who volunteered to join Washington's army at the north.

Colonel Woodford gave over his command

to Colonel Howe, of North Carolina, and after that he did little else than receive the praise he had so well earned. Everywhere he was feted and applauded, until even the tories began to come over to his way of thinking.

My company broke up and the men either went home or joined other commands, and I was given indefinite leave on account of my wound. Will, who held no commission, made ready to go with me to Judkins' Hall

Now that the fighting was over, Major Bullbeggor appeared to suffer acutely, and I made up my mind that the only thing that would save the old soldier's life would be for him to join the army in the north.

"It's no use, Dick, my boy," said he, the

day before I left him. "I have these pains a' shooting all through me and a vertigris in the skull. Why, I wouldn't be able to stand anything in that cold climate. This twitching of the nerves and numbing of the bones certainly means disintsgration, sir; yes, sir, it certainly does mean something. Go and get married, Dick, and try to get Will to join the army in the north. He will make a splendid soldier, for there's nothing so desperate and dangerous in a fight as a man crossed in love."

"But, Major," I said, "you know the army needs just such men as you to guide them in military affairs. It's your duty to go where your country calls for you when you are a soldier."

"I have a wife and six young children, Dick, all of them mostly ailing. I've tried Miranda Jones' spring medicine, and all of them have had Dr. McGuire bleed them until they could stand it no longer, but it didn't do any good. They are all dependent on me. Who would pay for their medicines if I should happen to fall ill and die?"

"They would probably be much better off if such an accident did happen to you," I answered, laughing. "It's about time you let them alone. I certainly think you ought to volunteer, or better still, raise a company with Will and myself in it. Then, with Sam and Snake to look out for us, we might operate to some advantage."

"I'll think of it, Dick. I'll think of it,

but I must go now to headquarters. Good-
bye!" And his lean hand closed upon mine
with a hearty grip. Then he took the bridle
of his mare from Snake and vaulted lightly
into the saddle. In a moment he and his
servant had disappeared around the corner
of the street.

I wended my way to the house where Will
and I were stopping and made ready for our
journey.

The next day about dusk we landed at the
Hall.

Of course it is needless for me to say much
about our welcome, but my poor mother's
joy at seeing us again was nothing to her
sorrow when Will had told the painful details of my affair with Harrison. After

Miss Carter heard the details of the fight she appeared to regard me with secret horror for a few days, but then I knew all women were much set against violence.

"But where is Mary now?" my mother asked of Will, after she had regained herself.

"Nothing could induce her to remain in sight of Dick," said Will, "so she sailed for England on one of Dunmore's vessels the day we entered Norfolk." And that was the last time I ever heard him mention my sister's name for years.

Rose was not a very joyous bride a couple of weeks later, but her tenderness and thoughtfulness made up for the lack of passionate love, which I felt sure she would develop as the **years** went by, and the memory of Harrison faded from her **mind.**

One day, about a month after we were married, I went to the stables to **see about** my horses getting their salt properly. **As I** stood at the stable window, looking out towards the slave quarters, I saw **Will Byrd** standing at the curve of the carriage drive, gazing steadily at a slave woman **who** held a shining black pickaninny in her arms. The slave woman sat **under a** tree and dangled some plaything over the child's face and crooned to it. The day was **cold,** and I thought it strange that the woman should sit there with the child, even though the little thing was carefully wrapped up in **a shawl.**

Will was evidently to my way of think-ing, for he gazed steadily at the child, and that strange look of deep sadness came over his face like I had noticed before in the hospital at Norfolk. Then he turned and walked slowly away, with his eyes cast upon the ground in front of him. Rose, who always looks after the people, then came out of the house and went straight toward the slave woman. She was evi-dently much upset at her carelessness in exposing the child so long to the weather, for she bent tenderly over it and kissed it, and then sent the woman away.

Ten minutes later, while I was walking through the grounds, attending to some necessary repairs, I saw the woman again, sitting now on the low stone fence that separated mine from the now deserted Harrison plantation. I walked up to her and reproved her sharply for keeping a year old child out so long in such cold weather.

"What is its name?" I asked.

"Marse Berk Harrison," she answered.

"Let me see him," I said, and I took hold of the child's arm to see if he was good and fat. It was a common practice to name slave children after the families to whom they belonged. Then I pinched the child's fat cheeks and a lot of black stuff, like burnt cork, came off on my hand, showing a white skin beneath it.

"Is he white?" I asked in astonishment.

"Oh, yes, Marse Judkins, he's white, but

we keeps him black, 'cause I has to take him so much with me to the quarters at the Hall."

"Who is his mother ?"

"'Deed I don't know, Marse Judkins Poor Miss Jude Berry over to the forks, I believe, but she's daid now this year gone— no two, last month—but her folks give him to me to raise, 'cause I lives at his uncles, an' they tole me to keep him black till he able to shift for hisself."

"Don't bring him to my quarters again," I said, and I handed her two pieces of gold. That is all. Perhaps it is enough. The whole horrible truth dawned upon me and I staggered away.

A week later Will insisted that he had

stayed out his visit at the Hall, and would join the army for the campaign against the British on Long Island, near New York. The same day Major Bullbeggor sent me an express that he would stop at the Hall and get Will and myself to help organize a company for Washington's army. He and Barron rode in a little later, accompanied by Snake in the Grass. The Major's face was most peculiarily marked and tattooed by the explosion of the grenadier's musket at the Great Bridge fight, and my mother hardly recognized him.

We made our preparations for departure within a few hours, and, accompanied by Sam and Snake, rode away from the Hall.

All the field hands were grouped at the

end of the carriage drive to wish us good-bye, while my sweet wife Rose and poor mother stood on the verandah and bade us a tearful farewell. God knows how my heart went out to that dear wife, as I saw her standing there with the sunshine playing on her hair and her eyes moist. But she smiled bravely and waved her handkerchief to us, and Snake nodded furiously in return until we rode slowly out of sight.

THE END.

Neely's Miscellaneous Books.

AMELIA E. BARR'S WORKS.
THUS RUNS THE WORLD AWAY. Cloth, $1.25.
WAS IT RIGHT TO FORGIVE? Cloth, $1.25.

OPIE READ'S WORKS.
ODD FOLKS. Cloth, $1.00 ; paper, 25c.
THE CAPTAIN'S ROMANCE. Cloth, $1.00 ; paper, 25c.

CAPT. CHARLES KING'S WORKS.
FORT FRAYNE. Cloth, $1.25 ; paper, 50c.
AN ARMY WIFE. Cloth, $1.25, 32 full-page Illustrations.
A GARRISON TANGLE. Cloth, $1.25 ; paper, 50c.
NOBLE BLOOD AND A WEST POINT PARALLEL. 50c.
TRUMPETER FRED. 50c. With full-page Illustrations.

MAX NORDAU'S WORKS.
THE AILMENT OF THE CENTURY. Cloth, $2.00.
THE SHACKLES OF FATE. Gilt Top, 50c.
HOW WOMEN LOVE. Cloth, $1.25.
THE RIGHT TO LOVE. Cloth, $1.50.
THE COMEDY OF SENTIMENT. Cloth, $1.50.
SOAP BUBBLES. Gilt top, 50c.

AN ALTRUIST. By Ouida. Gilt top, $1.00.
CHEIRO'S LANGUAGE OF THE HAND. Sixth Edition,
    $2.50.
IF WE ONLY KNEW AND OTHER POEMS. By Cheiro.
    Cloth, 50c.
THE BACHELOR AND THE CHAFING DISH. By Deshler
    Welsh. Illustrated. Cloth, $1.00.
THE LAND OF PROMISE. By Paul Bourget. Fully illus
    trated. Cloth, $1.00 ; paper, 25c.
NEELY'S HISTORY OF THE PARLIAMENT OF RELIG
    IONS. Over 1,000 pages, fully illustrated, $2.50.
DR. CARLIN'S RECEIPT BOOK AND HOUSEHOLD
    PHYSICIAN. Cloth, $1.00 ; paper, 50c.
LIFE AND SERMONS OF DAVID SWING. Cloth, $1.50 ;
    paper, 50c.
GIVING AND GETTING CREDIT. By F. B. Goddard.
    Cloth, $1.00.
THE ART OF SELLING. By F. B. Goddard. 50c.
A JOURNEY TO VENUS. By G. W. Pope. Cloth, $1.00,
    paper, 25c.
KERCHIEFS TO HUNT SOULS. By M. Amelia Fetche.
    Cloth, $1.00 ; paper, 25c.
FACING THE FLAG. By Jules Verne. Cloth, $1.00.
THAT EURASIAN. By Aleph Bey. Cloth, $1.25.
CORNERSTONES OF CIVILIZATION. Union College
    Practical Lectures (Butterfield Course). $3.00.
WASHINGTON, OR THE REVOLUTION. A drama, by
    Ethan Allen. 2 vols. Cloth, $3.00 ; paper, $1.00.

Neely's Popular Library.

Paper   -   Twenty-five Cents.

IN STRANGE COMPANY. By Guy Boothby.
    (With full-page half-tone Illustrations.)
RENTED—A HUSBAND. By Voisin.
THE NEW MAN AT ROSSMERE.
                By Mrs. J. H. Walworth.
A WOMAN'S MISTAKE, or, ON A MARGIN.
                By Julius Chambers.
THE ONE TOO MANY. By Mrs. Lynn Linton.

THE FAT AND THE THIN. By Emile Zola.
AT MARKET VALUE. By Grant Allen.
RACHEL DENE. By Robert Buchanan.
THE MINOR CHORD. By J. M. Chapple.
BOSS BART. By J. M. Chapple.
THE GATES OF DAWN. By Fergus Hume.
NANCE, A KENTUCKY BELLE. By Greene.
BITTER FRUITS. By M. Caro. (Fully Illustrated.)
ARE MEN GAY DECEIVERS?
                By Mrs. Frank Leslie.
NYE AND RILEY'S WIT AND HUMOR.
BILL NYE'S SPARKS.
LOVE AFFAIRS OF A WORLDLY MAN.
                By Mabelle Justice.
LOVE LETTERS OF A WORLDLY WOMAN.
                By Mrs. W. K. Clifford.
WAS IT SUICIDE? By Ella Wheeler Wilcox.
CLAUDEA'S ISLAND. By Esme Stuart.
WEBSTER'S PRONOUNCING DICTIONARY.
                (Illustrated.) 350 Pages.
THE DISAPPEARANCE OF MR. DERWENT.
                By Thomas Cobb.
SACRIFICED LOVE. By Alphonse Daudet.
THE MAHARAJAH'S GUEST. By Indian Exile.
THE LAST OF THE VAN SLACKS.
                By Edward S. Van Zile.
MARK TWAIN, HIS LIFE AND WORK.
THE MAJOR IN WASHINGTON.
SOCIAL ETIQUETTE. By Emily S. Bouton.

Neely's Library of
Choice Literature.

Paper, • Fifty Cents.

Neely's Library of
Choice Literature.

c.

The following Copyrighted Novels, published at **50c.** per copy, are now sold at **25c** each.